Books by Dee Henderson

Jennifer

AN O'MALLEY LOVE STORY

DEE HENDERSON

BETHANYHOUSE

a division of Baker Publishing Group
Minneapolis, Minnesota

© 2013 by Dee Henderson

Published by Bethany House Publishers
11400 Hampshire Avenue South
Bloomington, Minnesota 55438
www.bethanyhouse.com

Bethany House Publishers is a division of
Baker Publishing Group, Grand Rapids, Michigan

Printed in the United States of America

Library of Congress Cataloging-in-Publication Data is on file at the Library
of Congress, Washington, DC.

ISBN 978-0-7642-1112-6 (hardcover)
ISBN 978-0-7642-1155-3 (international trade paper)

This is a work of fiction. Names, characters, incidents, and dialogues are
products of the author's imagination and are not to be construed as real.
Any resemblance to actual events or persons, living or dead, is entirely
coincidental.

The internet addresses, email addresses, and phone numbers in this book
are accurate at the time of publication. They are provided as a resource.
Baker Publishing Group does not endorse them or vouch for their content
or permanence.

Cover design by Andrea Gjeldum

13 14 15 16 17 18 19   7 6 5 4 3 2 1

1

Her arms full of screaming, squirming boy, Dr. Jennifer O'Malley turned the corner of the Dallas hospital hallway and slammed open the ER doors with her shoulder. "Watch his burned hands!" In order to be heard over the angry cries of the child, her order had to cut like a sharp blade, and she pitched her voice accordingly. She headed toward the nearest empty exam area. She had a pretty good lock on the young boy from behind, and he wasn't going to reach anything but possibly her with his flailing feet and hands. It was the head butts that were going to make her lose her grip if they didn't get this situation quickly under control.

"Can he handle Amit?" the chief ER resident shouted, already pulling open the medicine cabinet door and grabbing for a syringe.

"Three milligrams. And follow it with two milligrams of Doram for the pain." The boy's bandaged hands were healing from second-degree burns and she was determined to not let him land one of his swings. She could feel the adrenaline in the child, fed by fear, anger, and pain. The boy managed to get a foot on the bed and shove it away.

The brush of a white coat across her shoulders combined with the whiff of perspiration and aftershave as a man reached over and around her to help hold the boy. "Easy, son. What happened?"

"His brother thought the bed restraints were some kind of punishment and undid them. Peter slid out of the bed, started running to find his mom—not knowing she's in the ICU—and we didn't catch up with him until he'd tried to put himself through a glass door."

"Yeah, that would make for a brutal afternoon."

The resident managed to get two clean injections into the boy's thigh. Within minutes Jennifer was holding a drowsy little boy, looking more for a place to lay his head than any further struggle.

"Okay?"

Jennifer nodded. The doctor behind her shifted the boy's weight fully back to her. She turned and placed the boy onto the bed, running a hand lightly across his cheek and brushing back his hair as he gave a last half sob. She was ready to share a few tears for him herself. "I'm sorry, honey. It's just not your week."

The boy was drifting further away with the meds. She lifted his left hand, saw the new damage under the disarray of the existing bandages, and looked over at his right. The skin was too fragile for the kind of impact he'd made with the glass door. "Carrie, page John. See if the OR can take him straight from here." He'd need the burns cleaned again and the open blisters tended, and that would have to be done with the boy under heavy sedation. She removed the existing bandages and used new gauze to protect the open wounds from drying out.

"His mom?"

At the query she glanced over and saw a face to go with the white coat for the first time. A tall man, sandy hair, blue eyes, and a rather nice face. "In the ICU burn unit, stable, thankfully. A cousin trying to be helpful brought Peter's brother in with her to visit him."

"Has the hospital assigned a family aide to assist the kids?"

"If they haven't, I'm next going to chew out some-one who probably signs my paycheck."

He smiled, and she thought she liked the smile. The ER hadn't been her normal terrain for close to six years now. The fact that she didn't know the man didn't surprise her. But she guessed from the garb he wore that he wasn't on his normal turf either. Those were surgical greens under the white coat.

Carrie rejoined them. "John said ten minutes, Jen. I'll take the boy up myself."

"Thanks." Jennifer was aware of her own adrena-line fading. She hadn't been expecting to step off the elevator and find herself in the middle of a chase to stop a desperate little boy looking for his mom.

She gently straightened his Superman pajamas, hoping he wouldn't be that mad at her when he woke up later. "He'll do for now. It was just bad luck they didn't open that door for him and let him keep run-ning."

"You took a couple knocks yourself. Let me see that eye."

She held still because the doctor was already prob-ing. "It's a bruise. And I'm late for rounds."

"It's definitely bruised." He glanced at the suckers in her lab-coat pocket. "What floor?"

"Oncology, pediatrics side."

"Go handle rounds. I'll back up Carrie to see our sleeping boy safely upstairs." But he paused her for a moment and offered a hand. "I'm Tom Peterson, by the way."

She took the offered hand, and hers disappeared in his. "Jennifer O'Malley."

"Nice to meet you, Jennifer."

She was sure now she liked the smile. And his timing. There wasn't much she could do but smile in reply. She headed back to work, wondering what other surprises were going to be in her day.

Tom Peterson relaxed in the staff break room, half dozing as he listened to a ball game on the radio behind him. The surgical wing had more silent stretches than most of the hospital floors. To the extent the surgery work could be scheduled, rotations started before seven a.m. and tended to end by midafternoon. There were still two cases coming through tonight, both relatively minor procedures, and he'd offered to be the one to stay so his partners could go on home.

He missed the hands-on general practice where he had begun his career, and young Peter this morning had reminded him of that time. Rarely did he encounter screamers anymore. The kid's hands had to have been really hurting.

"Tom, we're about ready," his chief surgical nurse said, appearing in the open break room door. "The anesthesiologist is beginning his countdown."

"Thanks, Gina." He stretched his arms out and flexed the tiredness away. "Gina?"

She paused in the doorway.

"Did you hear back from your sister?"

"Marla says Dr. O'Malley is in the same medical building as you and your partners, but on the third floor. She's one of the five partners in the LMR group. Kids that no one else can keep healthy, she does."

"Thanks."

"Just let me know before you go out with her so I can forewarn Marla. O'Malley's the sweetheart of the building, and there's a list floating around among her staff for who she should ideally date. Your name's not on it, by the way."

"Really?"

The door swung closed on her laugh. "Let's go, boss."

"This isn't good. You pulled your back helping the boy this morning."

The concerned words had Jennifer moving her hand away from the ache she had been rubbing deep in the muscles around her lower spine, and she straightened, trying not to show her wince. "Just twisted it a bit," she murmured, accepting the second cup the man carried. He must have spotted her long before she realized there was even someone else on this floor tonight, except the two nurses she had already spoken with. "Tom, was it?"

She knew it was, but there were protocols for first introductions becoming second ones when it was a guy she thought she might enjoy getting to know. She was thinking this was a situation that warranted all the protocols she could remember.

"Good memory. Heading somewhere in particular?"

He was definitely a surgeon, she decided, for he still wore booties over his shoes that spoke of the ultraclean scrub rooms lining this seventh floor. She picked up the two charts she had been reading. "Not really. My patients tend to spread across most of the hospital. Any hallway leads somewhere interesting at this point."

She specialized in wellness care for kids who were chronically or terminally ill. They already had the heart surgeon or oncologist in their lives. What they needed most was someone doing the preventive care so their colds and earaches didn't tip into something much worse for them. There was no such thing as a minor cold in a child who was already desperately ill.

Rather than walk, Tom chose to lean back against the wall beside the nurses' station. "My emergency eight o'clock started bleeding into his chest again, meaning the thoracic guy takes precedence over my starting work to rebuild the boy's jaw. And I've got a patient being medevaced in that won't be here for a couple hours. So this is me stalling, carrying around two cups of coffee, looking for someone who is equally bored or trying to stay awake."

She sipped at the lukewarm coffee he'd offered even as she studied him. She liked the fact there was a sense of calm patience about the man. He wasn't the typical type A personality she so often met on the surgical floor. "Who do you normally find at this time of night?"

"The guy in B-312 is recovering from a third heart attack, and he's always good for a story or two, even if it means I end up drinking both coffees because he's been banned from caffeine for life. And the janitor who handles the surgical floor can always be counted on for a decent baseball update when I'm bordering on desperate."

He was just about begging her to feel sorry for

him, and she found herself both amused and a touch charmed. She guessed him to be in his mid-thirties. To be working as a surgeon at this point in his career meant there hadn't been many slow hours in his life. The man wouldn't be doing surgery in this hospital, under this surgical department chief, without being one of the best in the nation at his job.

"How's the boy . . . Peter? Have you heard?" he asked.

"John doesn't think there was any lasting damage," she told him. She pointed toward the east hallway. She had a child coming out of a second round of ankle surgery who should be reaching recovery anytime now. Tom fell in step beside her. "We were able to give Peter a couple of minutes looking through the ICU glass to know we weren't lying about his mom being right upstairs. He's intent on getting better so he can sit with her. It breaks my heart, how adult a child can be at times."

"At least with youth comes a resiliency that adults rarely have. But, seriously—there was at least one casualty today. I think you need an ice pack before your back tightens up more and turns into a pretzel. You're not walking all that well at the moment."

"My leg is a bit numb," she conceded, "but I think it's more like twelve hours on my feet without the good pair of tennis shoes. I grabbed what I had nearby and ran this morning."

"Overslept?"

"In my defense, I got four hours of sleep before the alarm blared, I forgot what day it was, and I was halfway to the airport to pick up my sister before I realized my mistake. She doesn't come into town till tomorrow. Some days I don't think I'm handling this job as much as it's handling me."

"Been there. What you need is an excuse to take a couple of hours off work. Would you like to go out to dinner with me? The nurses will assure you I'm single, relatively interesting, and have a mom in town who still keeps me in line and a gentleman." He glanced down with a rueful smile. "I promise I clean up into something better than scrubs and booties."

"I admit, the booties are kind of cute."

"Tomorrow—say, seven o'clock? You can introduce me to your sister, we can duck out for an hour and eat, and then I'll have you safely home so she can pester you with all kinds of questions about your date."

"As intriguing as that sounds, I have to say no. Kate is not the sister I spring a date on if I expect to actually leave the house. She's a cop, and not inclined to trust an unknown guy with her baby sister."

He laughed. "I already like her."

Her pager went off. She looked at the text and headed toward the elevators, glancing over her shoulder at him as she dropped the empty coffee cup in the nearest trash can. "Got a medevac incoming. Sorry."

"Promise you'll walk by this floor again during your odd hours around here?"

"I think that's a safe assumption for even a Texas surgeon to make."

"You're not Texan, I'm thinking."

"Chicago, south side." The elevator doors closed before she could add, *youngest of seven.*

The elevator rose swiftly toward the roof of the building. She didn't think her large and inclined-to-meddle family would slow him down, but it never hurt to at least mention them early on. Her three brothers tended to be very interested—in a check-out-his-background kind of way—about any guy who thought dating her would be a good idea.

She suspected Tom Peterson would see her family more as a challenge than an obstacle. He had that air of confidence about him, and, surprisingly, she was looking forward to finding out. Her self-imposed sabbatical of a year off dating might be coming to an end in a rather unexpected way.

She hurried through the receiving area and out into the warm night air on the roof as the sound of the approaching helicopter overtook the silence. Caution still had its merits, she told herself. It had saved her from starting a few relationships where she would have ended up with a broken heart.

She wouldn't be finding extra reasons to be on the surgical floor, hoping to run into him again. If Tom wanted to get to know her, he'd have to make the effort. As a final protocol in deciding what a guy was really like, waiting always worked. She loved her job too much to let just anyone crowd into the time she spent with the kids she helped.

A downward rush of air had her covering her eyes as the medical flight landed. Her evening looked like it would be long, and she didn't mind it a bit. She'd dreamed about being a doctor since she was a young girl, and living that dream now was exhilarating. The rest of what she dreamed for her future—she still had plenty of time in her life to see it come true too.

2

In the medical building adjoining the hospital that housed the clinic where Jennifer spent most of her time, the day had passed with a steady stream of patients. "Let's schedule a follow-up for Annie in three weeks, and new blood work panels in two." Jennifer passed the paperwork to the scheduling nurse, the *no bill* notation at the bottom for this visit one of the few things she could do to help the family. "That sound all right with you, Annie?" She rested her hand over the child's on the wheelchair's armrest.

"Yeth!"

The twelve-year-old had less control over her speech than most children her age. Jennifer interpreted the reply in light of the smile the girl gave her. She smiled back as she leaned over to help with the girl's jacket. Three weeks would sound like a vacation to one of her favorite patients. The stroke had done so much damage, it was going to be a long-term task to get this fun-loving child back on track.

"Just one prescription for you this time," Jennifer announced. "I want to see the color of green on those tennis shoes next month, from all the running around you did on your new backyard grass. You can chase Elliot to your heart's content."

"He might leth me cath him."

Jennifer shared a laugh with the girl. "You'll tickle him if you catch him, I think."

Jennifer looked over at Annie's mom. "She's doing really well," she repeated, knowing it never hurt to re-iterate the good news in situations like this one. "Her muscle tone is improving, and her ability to balance is much better. If you're comfortable keeping up the pool routine, I think it's doing everything we hoped it might."

"I will. She loves it when we go exercising together."

The girl nodded her agreement.

"You're comfortable with the new physical thera-pist?" Jennifer asked Annie.

"Like Tish."

"Annie hit it off with Trish. They're a good team," her mom agreed.

"That's good to hear. Her lungs are clear, and there's not even a bit of congestion to watch. If nothing comes up before then, I'll see you again in three weeks."

"Thanks, Dr. O'Malley."

"Call me, here or at home, if you have any concerns."

Annie's father, having gone to get the car, reappeared. Jennifer waved a final good-bye as she watched the three leave. There had been progress, enough to be visible now, and improvements were still coming. Jennifer would rest on that good news, since she could do nothing to reverse the stroke or the surgery needed afterward.

The waiting room was crowded with kids, since all her partners were holding office hours today. Jennifer glanced at her watch as she headed back toward her office. Her day was flowing by smoothly, and she was determined to enjoy that rare luxury. She idly wondered if Tom was having a decent day too, and thought again about her decision not to find an excuse to return to the hospital's surgical floor. She didn't regret the decision, she concluded, but she did wonder what was taking him so long to search her out. It had been ten days since they had shared coffee together, and their paths hadn't crossed since then.

She found it amusing, the thought that he might be doing a bit of waiting too, just to see if she would be the one who came chasing. Mid-thirties, nice face to look at, doctor, single—he probably got pursued a lot. He needed a challenge. She'd never been one to be part of the crowd. Any O'Malley would tell him that.

She pulled the chart for her next patient. *Gregory*. The little guy was a ball of energy. She proceeded down the hall to exam room two.

"Jennifer."

She paused to let her chief nurse catch up with her and accepted the call slip. She tried not to let the sinking sensation in the pit of her stomach show on her face as she read the note. "Tell Linda to come on in. I'll see Veronica as soon as they can get here."

Four months of working to get Veronica strong enough for surgery and it was going to be postponed once again because of a fever. She could only hope it wasn't as bad as the note suggested it might be.

"Should I give Dr. Travers a heads-up as well?" Marla asked.

"I'll do it once we've got the blood cultures in the works. Alert his nurse for me so he doesn't leave to-night without us touching base."

Marla nodded and then left to make the calls.

Jennifer pushed the note into her pocket. It wasn't easy to get ahold of her emotions, but she did it because she couldn't carry them with her right now. She took a breath, cleared her face, relaxed her shoulders, and opened the exam room door. "Hi, Gregory. How's my buddy today?"

The five-year-old boy perched on the exam table threw his hands up in the air, and the balsa-wood airplane he was aiming landed against the wall, the teddy bear hit the floor, and his face lit up in laughter. "Take it off! You're taking it off today."

She grinned. "I am indeed."

In their private little hello, she tickled his toes on the foot without the cast and glanced over at the boy's mom. "I gather he was ready to come in early for a change."

"He was encouraging me to drive faster."

The cast he wore to keep his ankle together after three rounds of surgery would become just a special boot today. "First we check all these other toes and elbows and fingers, then I'm taking you over to see Jim, and this hard little cast is going bye-bye," she promised. He had a brittle-bone disease that snapped his bones like they were twigs. The damage to his ankle from simply running and falling had nearly been unfixable.

She warmed up the stethoscope in her hand. His doctors were finally making some progress in halting the bone disease's progress, but the drug combinations being used left the boy's liver badly stressed. He was prone to catching every bug that came around. She listened to his chest and thought he was no worse than his last visit, but not clear either. "Has Mr. Cough come back to visit?"

Gregory shook his head.

"How about Mr. Sniffles?"

"Can I have a sucker if he visited just a little?"

She offered her lab-coat pocket. "There's every flavor to choose from this time."

"Grape."

She handed over the sucker. "So Mr. Sniffles just kind of passed through?"

Gregory nodded.

She checked his ears and throat, then got him to hold still while she repeated the temperature check her nurse had done. Her instincts were telling her Gregory was heading for a chest cold, for the minor signs hadn't dissipated in the last week. "All done, Gregory. Let's go have this cast removed."

"Can I ride in the blue bomber?"

"You may."

Rather than picking him up from under the arms,

out of habit she moved him by sliding her hands under him and lifting him up from the exam table and over into the blue, child-sized powered wheelchair. A normal grip would risk breaking his ribs. "Remember, Mr. Blue goes faster on the downslopes."

"I remember."

She held the door open for him, glad that at least this part of his doctor's visits was considered fun. It didn't hurt either that he was best buddies with his bone doctor.

She followed the boy toward the lab doors, hanging back a few paces from him so she could talk privately with his mom while they walked. "The blood work is still in range, so there are no new worries on that front. His docs are ecstatic at the rate of bone-density growth they're seeing. I'm worried about the cold that never fully clears, but at this point more medication seems counterproductive. It's something that will just have to be watched."

"I'll bring him back in if the congestion gets any worse."

"Good. Have you noticed anything that has you concerned, anything new in symptoms?"

"He's been stable, which is a nice relief."

"For both of us."

Jennifer moved to open the door for Gregory, and

the boy powered ahead in the chair to join the doctor who was already working to size the new boot.

"He wants it off today, Jim."

"So he tells me. I think we can oblige him. Thanks for shooting over the film. Do you want to do the honors or shall I?"

"I get to be the one to remove the boot when therapy is done."

"Okay, then let's get this show on the road. Do you want to watch, Gregory? Or play your favorite video game and ignore what I'm doing to your foot until I'm all done?"

"Wanna watch," Gregory insisted.

"Then let me show you how this is done," the doctor said, smoothly transferring him from the chair to the table with his hands under the boy. He set to work arranging the protective mat. "So tell me more about this backyard fort of yours. I hear it's a masterpiece."

Jennifer's pager vibrated. She looked down and saw the text message that Veronica and Linda had arrived.

She coded a reply, then looked over at Gregory's mom. "After Jim fits the special boot he'll wear, why don't you come back to my office and we'll talk about what makes sense for physical therapy this summer. I'll have copies of his latest lab work and X-rays for you as well. When you see the specialist in Maryland next month, he'll use them as the new baselines."

"I'll do that."

Jennifer exchanged a wave with Gregory and headed back to her office to meet Linda and her daughter Veronica.

Marla met her in the back hallway of the practice. "Veronica is in exam room six. She was fine last night but woke with a bad headache, developed a fever mid-morning, and vomited twice in the last hour. I've already called over to see if pediatrics has a bed available."

"She's deathly afraid of the cardiac unit since her friend passed away. Ask them to give me a bed in orthopedics if they have to."

"Will do."

Jennifer tapped on the exam room door and then opened it. She offered a smile to Linda, then looked to her patient. "I hear you're not feeling so good today, Veronica. What's happening, honey?"

Jennifer clicked off her desk light, picked up her briefcase and the box she planned to drop into the outgoing mail, and stepped out into the quiet hall. Gregory had forgotten his bear. She'd found it tucked in her office couch cushions and had boxed it to mail back to him. Her partners in the practice, along with the nurses and support staff who worked with them, had all left for the night.

Going home didn't appeal. She turned the lights on in the waiting room and sat down at a child-high table in a matching chair. She searched for a piece or two to fit into a jigsaw puzzle. Friday nights in Dallas didn't seem much different from Friday nights in Chicago, where she'd grown up and done her residency. There always came an hour when the work for the week was done and a few hours of downtime stretched ahead unfilled. A movie didn't appeal either. Maybe she should go buy herself an ice cream.

"I hear you had a tough day."

She looked up.

Tom was leaning against the glass entry doors to the practice, watching her. She was surprised to see him here at this time of night. She knew he had offices in the same medical building, but surgeons tended to work the very early hours of the day over at the hospital.

"One of my patients developed a fever," she said. "Her surgery likely will have to be postponed, and she can't afford the delay. She's got a mass the size of a walnut trying to grow in her chest and it's pressing on her esophagus."

Veronica had been a patient since the girl was three years old, and every year brought something new to fight. The growths were not malignant, didn't have a known cause, and didn't respond to treatment. The first one had appeared beneath her heart and nearly pinched off a major artery by the time it could be surgically removed. The second had affected her right lung. The third had appeared in the soft tissue behind her knee. This latest one had hit when she was too weak from other medical problems to handle the surgical procedure. The poor kid just couldn't get a break. "I'm hopeful the fever is only the flu." But she was worried, and it was one of the reasons she couldn't settle tonight.

She held up a hand and offered Tom a puzzle piece. "Come on, help me out."

He walked over. Rather than risk a child-sized chair, he sat down on the carpet.

He worked on the puzzle with her, filling in the puppy ears.

He leaned into her space with another puzzle piece. "Want to get a bite to eat with me?"

She glanced at him, but his attention was on orienting a furry piece of white. "Maybe."

"You should say yes. I know all kinds of good places to eat that are still open at this time of night."

Jennifer nudged him over so she could work on the puppy's eyes. "I may need to come back to check on Veronica if her fever gets worse."

"Not a problem." He finished the ears and got to his feet. "Come on, Jennifer."

He offered her a hand up from the child's chair. She didn't think her legs would hold her and shifted her hand to grasp his arm. She shook off the weakness with an apologetic laugh. "Sorry."

He was frowning. "Your back is still bothering you."

"Just at the odd moments when I act younger than my age." She gestured to the short chair. She picked up her briefcase and felt no further twinge even holding its weight. "Do you know a place that does a Chicago-style pizza? I'm getting desperate for a taste of home."

"That's a challenge." He thought a moment and nodded. "But one I think I can meet."

He was keeping the conversation and meal low-key, and she appreciated that. The tables were small and round, squeezed around the cramped edges of the café. There were pizzas on the menu called New York and California, and even a challenger from Ohio. Tom had ordered two Chicago-styles, and they were massive deep-dish offerings. The pizza arrived on paper plates with plastic forks and knives.

"Close enough to the real thing?"

"It's not bad," she agreed happily after the first couple of bites, wondering how she had not discovered this place before. "Actually, it's rather good. Okay, you've heard about my day. How was yours?"

"A kid skateboarding tried to jump down a flight of concrete stairs and ended up putting his knee square into a riser with the full weight of his body behind the contact. I spent most of the day assisting while Dr. Sandover put the puzzle of broken bones back into some semblance of order."

"Was it successful?"

"He's got a chance, which is about as far as anyone wants to predict with this one. He'll likely end up as the first fourteen-year-old in his school with an artificial knee." Tom rose to get them more napkins. "Talk to me about how a Chicago native ended up in Texas," he said when he returned and handed her several. "You grew up in Chicago. You went to medical school there too?"

"I did. I came to Texas because I wanted Dr. Marish as my pediatrics mentor ever since I read the book she wrote, *Thriving Kids*, and there was an opening in the residency program here. I gambled on liking her enough to make up for the move."

"I hope Texas has grown on you a bit more since then."

"It's been giving its best shot. I do like it here. But I miss home."

"I remember you mentioned your sister was coming to town. Did you have a good visit?"

She grinned at the memory of what it was like having Kate around her place for the all-too-brief thirty-six-hour visit. That's all they'd been able to squeeze in given Kate's schedule. "We had a great time. Think energy explosion and lots of laughter, and you'll come close."

Because it was easier to show what was unusual about her life than try to explain it, she reached for her billfold and unzipped the back compartment. A cascade of photos slid out into her hand, the majority of them current and former patients, but toward the back she found a few of the snapshots she sought. She held one of them out to him.

"The O'Malleys. There are seven of us, but it's not exactly a traditional family. We're all orphans. Kate, who I mentioned," she said, pointing her out, "and that's Marcus. Stephen. Lisa. Rachel. Jack. We sort of adopted each other. Legally changed our last names, became our own family."

He looked at the picture, looked at her, and then looked back at the picture. "Wow." He shook his head. "I'd say something about how creative a solution that is, and how strong the desire is to be part of a family, but I'd just sound even more stupid than *wow*. Really?"

"We might not share a blood connection, but the group is as strong as if we do. We've been together twenty-plus years now, and I don't think a single one of us regrets it. We're constantly stepping in and out of each other's lives."

He smiled and handed the picture back. "You look happy in that photo, and I can hear the joy in your voice just mentioning them. I envy you a bit—that closeness you have with them."

"Only child?"

"Hmmm. And have regretted it for a decade."

"Why's that?"

"Mom wants grandkids."

She laughed at his rueful tone.

"One of the trials of being the only son. I can't blame her. Family matters. The older I get, the more I enjoy my parents' company, and them mine, I think."

"They live here in town?"

He nodded. "They do. I see them at least a couple of times a week, talk to them even more often. Dad's a research doctor, which is where I got the love for this work in the first place. They're getting to be in frail health and can no longer travel like they once did, but otherwise are doing well." He gestured to the larger stack of photos. "May I see?"

"Sure." She handed them over. "My kids," she explained, suddenly feeling awkward about the personal connection she made with so many of her patients.

He laughed at the animal costumes. "You do believe in laughter being good medicine." He turned one of the birthday-party pictures toward her.

"Boredom is a problem when you have to spend days and nights and more days in a hospital ward."

"No need to explain. When I worked the pediatrics floor, I was thrilled when there was someone like you around to keep their spirits up."

She finished her pizza while she watched him turn photos.

He'd had the tact not to immediately ask how she'd ended up an orphan, how her parents had died, and she quietly gave him points for that. Some memories still hurt when they were stirred up, and the memory of the night the drunk driver hit her parents' car was still painful. The added hurt that there had been no one stepping forward to take her in after her parents had been killed only intensified the pain.

She knew how rough life could be for a child when

things went wrong, when the promise of two parents and a stable home disappeared. It was one of the reasons she was so determined to help kids who were ill and to do whatever she could to brighten their days. The orphanage, Trevor House, had given her the O'Malleys, along with her focus on becoming a doctor.

She gestured to one of the photos. "My sister Kate was the one who thought up the sheriff's badges for those who were fighting cancer."

"You mentioned she was a cop?"

Jennifer nodded.

"I think I would like her a great deal." Tom turned one of the photos to show her. "Can I keep this one? You have two prints here."

She blushed, for it was one of her smiling at the camera, blue twinkle stars hand-painted on her cheeks and silver-glitter eye shadow highlighting her eyes. She shrugged. "Sure. If you want."

He slipped it into his shirt pocket. "I've watched you with the kids. I think you are a doctor because you love kids first and enjoy medicine second."

"Probably so."

"No desire to start your own family?"

"When the time is right," she finally said, not sure what to do with the question. She shrugged again.

"If I end up waiting too long, I'm not opposed to adopting."

He finished his pizza. "Loving kids as well as treating them makes being a doctor much more of a lifestyle than a career for you, I'm guessing."

"Yes, I think it is."

"I like that fact." He nodded toward the front counter. "Care for dessert?"

"I'll pass and suggest a walk. It's a nice evening out, even if it's pretty late."

"Good idea." He stood and gathered up their plates, carrying them to the trash. "Let's wander toward downtown and enjoy the lights?"

Jennifer smiled. "Please."

The fountain by city hall was brightly lit. They walked toward it in mutual agreement, the sound of the cascading water welcoming in the night. She took a seat on the wide encircling bench. The coins at the bottom of the shallow pool sparkled, and she pitched a penny upward, watching it circle in the air before landing with a soft plop in the water.

Tom dug out a handful of change from his pocket and held it out to her.

She carefully selected another penny. "Why haven't you gotten married and given your mom those grand-kids?"

He studied the penny balanced on his finger, then smiled and sent it spinning into the pool. "Some things in life don't get better when they're rushed. Marriage is one of those things. Do you know how many people get married who aren't even friends yet?"

"That's a scary thought." She sorted through his change and chose a dime. "I think I'm more interested in just not being the first in my family to do something. Definitely not being the first to get married."

She watched the dime land in the water with a small splash. "We're a close family. And there's rock-ing the boat, and then there's tipping it over. I'm not the one who normally does any tipping. That would be Kate occasionally, when her work gets her shot at. Or sometimes Jack, because he fights fires a little too close at times when someone has to be rescued and he gets himself singed. One of us getting married would feel like a pretty big shift." She selected another penny from his handful of change and sent it sailing through the air, spinning in the moonlight. "I've got to remember this. My kids would get a blast out of flipping coins into the water."

He laughed and offered her another dime. "I'm

beginning to appreciate the kid still in you every time you let her show her face."

"I'm normally too responsible, but then there are moments like this . . ." She stopped the slide of change into her hand and closed his fist around the coins. "Take me home, Tom. It was a nice pizza, a good walk, and now I'd like to be home by midnight."

He studied her face, then smiled. "Can we do this again? Maybe not the pizza, but the time? I enjoyed myself, Jennifer."

"So did I. Which is why you're taking me home before midnight."

"Cautious, wise, and something else . . . someone is calling you tonight? Family perhaps?"

"Let's just say I'm aware it's Friday night, and most O'Malleys don't respect sane hours when they have a free minute to call."

"You'll be safely home before midnight."

"You're laughing at me."

"With you. I think I like your family already. Miles away, and still they keep you on your best behavior."

"Just try being the youngest of seven for a while. It's a very different world than you can even imagine."

3

Jennifer began to look forward to the slices of time when Tom would track her down at the office. Or she'd linger around the hospital, taking evening rounds when she knew he was scheduled for late surgery. It became a pattern for their friendship—walking together when the workday ended, sharing the occasional meal or coffee at the end of their stroll to continue their conversation.

It was raining on Tuesday night when she ducked out from under the restaurant's front-door canopy and hurried toward his car pulling up to the curb. He leaned over to open the door for her. "This is sure not the clear weather that was forecasted."

"I'd say." It had put an end to their usual walk. The pizza tonight had been more upscale than the first place he had taken her, but she couldn't say it was better. She settled in as Tom pulled out into traffic.

"So are you planning to work this weekend?" Tom asked.

Jennifer tried to remember the calendar on her desk. "I'm off, not even a pager, but Saturday morning is planned."

"Would you like to do something together? I was thinking we eventually ought to actually schedule something." He glanced over at her, then back to the wet pavement.

She smiled. "I happen to like spontaneous. There are less dress-up decisions and pacing involved."

He glanced over again, looking amused. "True. But it's hard to get tickets to a ball game or concert on the spur of the moment. Let's find a newspaper and see what's going on around town this weekend."

"I'd lean toward the ball game in that list of options."

Tom idled at the light before the turn toward her home. "Do you want to call it a night yet? It's still early. You could come by and see the house I've been talking about, and I'll find us a movie to watch."

"Sure, I'd like to see your place. Just have me home by midnight."

He turned south rather than north. "Does your family actually call you that late?"

"Occasionally. It's more the fact I'm too old for late nights. I need my sleep."

He laughed. "There are priorities that come with the job, sleep being high on the list. I'm just fortunate I don't have surgery scheduled for tomorrow or I'd be begging off myself to call it a night."

Intrigued, Jennifer wandered around Tom's home, putting together her image of him from work and from their conversations as they walked with the tangible things he had collected. The place was much more Spartan than she had expected. The furnishings were comfortable, guy-sized, and the colors on the walls well chosen. But those walls were mostly bare, the tabletops clear. She found stacks of artwork leaning against a wall in the dining room and a wonderful collection of blown-glass globes and paperweights, still wrapped, in a box by the fireplace hearth. Tom had moved in, but he hadn't yet finished making it home.

That he was a reader she had known from the variety of subjects that came up during their conversations, but seeing the shelves of books he had collected reminded her of that fact. The number of volumes spoke of a man comfortable with his life and not needing to fill every evening with people to be content. She liked that about him.

She lingered at the shelves, scanning titles, forming an impression about what had caught his interest over time. The books on medical matters were expected, the ones on the Old West were not, and the fiction section was vast. She saw several books about God and the Bible and wondered at them.

Tom joined her, carrying two mugs of hot chocolate topped with whipped cream. She accepted one with a quiet thanks, for the rain had left her a bit chilled, and waved a hand toward the rooms she had explored. "I like your home. It has potential."

"I agree with the potential. This place needs time and energy, neither of which I've given it yet." He knelt and pushed open a cabinet to search out a DVD option. "That was one of the reasons I wanted you to see it, so expectations would settle quickly into something closer to reality."

She leaned against the side of the cabinet and watched him. "I think it's the pictures and artwork.

I tend to think in quantity. You have almost bare walls. Nice paint-color choices, but not much on them yet."

That he had settled for a couple of bedrooms, a home office, along with a kitchen seldom used, reflected where he spent his time. The home office was the most put-together space she had seen. Her place had more the feel of a home, but it wasn't fundamentally all that different.

"My mother would agree with you. When the rain stops, I'll show you the backyard and the large deck. It's the reason I bought this place, more than the house itself. One day when life is more settled, I'll turn my attention to at least getting the artwork hung." He held up a DVD. "Season three of *Next Generation*?"

She studied the show listing, then nodded. "Perfect."

He turned on the stack of equipment next to his television, slid in the DVD, and kicked on the surround-sound speakers.

A scan of the room gave her several options. She headed toward comfort and sank into the leather couch. She kicked off her shoes and curled her feet up under her.

"How's the pain tonight?"

"What?"

"You've got a nice tell—you rub what hurts. You've

41

rubbed that right knee at least three times tonight since we went for dinner." He settled into the big chair beside the couch and picked up the remote. "Can I at least get you something for it?"

"I wasn't aware I was doing it. It's just bruised. I lost my balance and turned into the corner of an exam table this afternoon."

"Ouch." He passed her the remote. "Set the volume where it's comfortable. We need popcorn." He got up and reached for his mug. "Want a popcorn bag of your own? I'm pretty good at the microwave kind."

"Sure."

The show began while Tom was gone. She relaxed back into the couch. This wasn't quite the ending of the day she had expected, but she wouldn't have traded it for other options. She liked sharing space and time with him in a way she hadn't thought she would. This was the real man behind the layers, not one trying overly hard to impress her, and she liked what she was finding.

There wasn't so much an *I'm dating him* feel to the relationship as a solid friendship, and it made life so much easier to stay relaxed and normal around him. She was wise enough to see that Tom was planning to one day attempt to turn the relationship into something more, but he wasn't being overly intense about it. As a middle ground, they seemed to have hit the right note.

She caught herself rubbing her knee again. The bruise ached. She had to get better at covering her tells. Tom had been watching her more closely than she realized to have noticed it tonight.

"Do you remember this episode?"

She glanced over as Tom came back in with the popcorn. She accepted a bag. "Vaguely. If I'm remembering correctly, it's pretty good."

"I like repeats. I can enjoy the good parts again."

Tom turned off the television and ejected the DVD. "You're half asleep."

Jennifer caught herself beginning to nod off and stretched as she uncurled from her position on the couch. "Guilty. I'm conditioned to fall asleep when I stop moving. I don't often sit for a couple of hours." She yawned as she saw the time. It was comfortably late, but she felt a nice kind of relaxed. She glanced toward the dark windows. "I think the rain stopped."

"About an hour ago," Tom agreed.

He didn't look tired, and she wondered where he got so much energy. She felt dead at this time of night.

He offered her a hand up from the couch. "I'll give you a ride home, and you can go curl up under the covers and finish the rest of that dream. You were smiling as you drifted off."

His hand was warm where hers was still a bit cold, and she let hers linger in his for a moment, enjoying the contact. "Memories. The last time I got a relaxing evening like this, my sister Rachel was in town. She's always good for a hug and a few hours of peaceful downtime. With Kate it tends to be more of a whirl-wind of activity flowing by. I love that too. They are just very different visits."

She stretched again and worked the stiffness out of her back. "Take me home. We'll do this again some night at my place. I can probably be talked into trying to make brownies or something to go with the show."

"Now you're talking." He reached over to remove something from her hair. "The pillow is shedding, I think. A hazard of new purchases." He showed her the small white tag.

"Thanks."

She was more interested in the casual touch, the fact he hadn't moved his hand away, than in his words. Half a step forward on her part and she could get a hug, but he wasn't going to close the distance without her doing so. She smiled and stepped back. "I was thinking, if you're free, you should come join me Saturday morning. Say eight?"

"What's planned?"

She laughed. "You sound kind of suspicious. It's easier to show you than explain. Plan old jeans, and carrying stuff, and you'll be good to go."

The practice didn't have scheduled patients on Saturday, but most of the staff was in today, using the morning to clear away paperwork while painters came and went. Exam rooms were being repainted, and new carpet was going in the next day. Jennifer took over the larger of the two conference rooms once the furniture was removed, taking advantage of this opportunity for more interesting plans for the space.

Tom maneuvered through the door carrying the second of the boxes from her car trunk. "Did you say 'party' with a lower or uppercase *P*?"

"I only know how to do one kind." She searched the box to find the white tablecloth with the happy birthday banner folded up inside. "There it is. I was getting worried I'd forgotten a box. Can you get the cake or should I come down to the car to help?"

"I can handle it."

He picked up one of the small pillows. There were baskets of them around the room now, the six-by-six-inch soft pillows in a rainbow of colors. "You made these."

"Over the years. It's called a pillow fight, kid-style. As long as the cake and punch are covered, they can't do much damage."

"Can adults join in?"

"After the party is over."

"I can see I'm just getting used for my muscles."

"Want to blow up balloons?" She offered one of them to him.

"I'll go get the cake."

"I thought you'd opt out of the hot-air job." She started blowing into a balloon.

"I think you're going to enjoy this morning more than the kids."

"Probably. They arrive in an hour. Get back to work."

He grinned. "Yes, ma'am."

The whiteboard had become an outlined mural, waiting for the kids to color it in.

"Your cowboy is crooked," Jennifer pointed out, studying the sketch.

Tom stepped back from the board to get a better perspective. "He broke in too many horses and leans when he stands."

She laughed. "That will work." She looked around the room. "Mural board, balloon animals, pillow fight kid-style, and then cake and punch. I think we're ready."

Tom set down the marker he was using. He picked up one of the long red balloons. "You have enough balloons to equip an army."

She peered into the plastic trash bag beside her. "Probably."

"How many are coming to this party?"

Jennifer looked over at her partner, who was setting out the plates and paper cups. "What's the current count, Amy? Twelve?"

"Maybe fourteen, if Kim and her brother come."

Tom twisted the balloon into a circle hat and plopped it on Jennifer's head. "I need to run upstairs for a minute and get a file before I return a call. Anything else you need before the kids arrive?"

"I'm set. Thanks for the help."

"Oh, I'll be back. I'm not going to do all this work, then miss out on the fun."

By noon the party was breaking up. Standing in the doorway to see her kids safely off, Jennifer accepted a child's hug, whispered a happy birthday and got a giggle in return. She offered a handshake to the girl's brother, a patient of hers in his own right, and the one who had suggested the party. "See you later, Franklin."

"Bye, Doc. This was nice. She had a good time."

"I did too."

She turned to the next child. Cake icing had mixed with face paint on Gregory's face. She wiped it off, exchanged his version of soft high fives, and watched, pleased as he headed toward his mom to show off the picture Franklin had helped him create, the special boot he wore not slowing him down at all. The party was a huge success if measured by the kids' fun.

Jennifer surveyed the room after the last child was out the door and reached for a box to start the cleanup. The best parties inevitably left the most bits and pieces behind. She scooped up little pillows to save for the next pillow fight.

Tom was collapsed on the floor in the middle of the conference room. She stepped over him and reached for another of the pillows. "Admit it. I throw a super party." He'd returned as promised, giving her his entire morning.

"Yes, you do throw a super party." He reached for

one of the pillows and tossed it to her. "The kids had a good time." His smile faded. "How many of them are cancer survivors?"

She picked up a balloon that now looked more like a blob than an animal. "Most of them."

She sat down on the floor beside him and brushed a piece of cake icing off his sleeve. "Thanks for helping today. It was useful having another guy around. They seemed to like you."

"I was surrounded by giggling, adoring little girls who wanted to meet the doctor their beloved Jennifer talks about. It was good for my ego, if not my social skills—I have no idea what most of them were talking about when it came to things they liked."

"You're getting old."

"You don't have to sound so amused about that." He sat up, took the balloon and untwisted it to fix it back to a recognizable animal. "I talked to your partner Steve about seeing patients with you on occasion," he mentioned, his focus on the balloon.

Jennifer blinked at the casual comment, then smiled at him. "Did you? What did he say?"

"He laughed, but then said he didn't see any problems with the idea, since I've already got the insurance coverage with my own practice. Give him a week or so to do the paperwork and I'm an affiliated member of your partnership, free to stop by anytime. I was thinking some Monday when you do office appointments and my surgery schedule is free, I'd come hang around awhile and meet some more of your kids. A few months from now, if you catch a cold or something and need a day off work, maybe I'll know your patients well enough to cover appointments for you."

"I admit I like the idea. I'm just surprised you would want to shift some of your time like that."

"I miss general practice, the ear infections and throat tickles and skinned knees from falls. And I'm tired of seeing you only when our work schedules give us a few hours off in common. This way I solve both problems." He turned his head and studied her a bit more closely. "What are you thinking about so hard?"

She didn't want to say, for it would simply make her blush more. She turned over the box she held and buried him with little pillows.

4

It had been too wet to appreciate Tom's backyard and deck during her last visit to his home. Tonight it wasn't a problem. Jennifer stepped up onto the deck, back from their walk through his neighborhood park. "I can see why you love this. It's gorgeous out here."

"I think so," Tom replied, joining her at the low railing.

The yard was large but secluded by a privacy fence. The ring of orchard trees was not something often found in Texas. It spoke of the time and energy Tom hadn't yet given the inside of his home. She understood why he had begun here.

The night was pleasant, the stars out, the moon only a sliver. Someone nearby had cooked out for dinner, and the faint smell of charcoal and grilled chicken lingered in the air. Jennifer moved over to settle on a padded deck chair while Tom went inside for cold drinks. "Make mine diet if you can, please," she called after him.

Jennifer took the glass Tom returned with, offered a thank-you, and leaned her head back. "Take away some of the city lights and this would be a wonderful place to stargaze."

"Early on, after I had gotten the house, I would often sit out here and daydream. I haven't done enough of that recently." He relaxed into a chair beside her and set aside his own soda. "I miss quiet evenings like this. Life gets too busy. I let it get too busy." He reached across the space between them to touch her hand. "Did you hear back from your brother?"

"Yes." She smiled at the memory of their conversation. Jack had managed to catch her just as she was trying to touch-up paint a wall she had gashed with a shelf she'd been moving. The call had turned into a family gab session, and that wall was still not repainted. "We're going to try for the July Fourth weekend to get everyone together. If I juggle things right, I can get the time off work."

"It sounds like it will be a good time."

"It will be. What about you? Did you catch your parents in?"

"Dad's presentation got moved up, but I still got a few minutes of his time to pass on my comments before he left. I wish I was going to be there to hear it in person. Lunch was great—Mom had fixed her fabulous pumpkin pie." He turned to look over at her. "I meant to save you a piece, but I have to admit I ate it."

She laughed. "I can see your priorities. I'm glad you're close to your dad. That has to be something he appreciates too."

She studied the stars stretched out overhead, so many of them, in so many different shades of brightness. "I need to be getting home," she murmured, but she didn't move. This was too peaceful to want to abandon. Housework was waiting for her, and bills to pay. She'd promised herself she would at least get her grocery shopping list written tonight if not the shopping itself. She had settled for oatmeal this morning, as she was out of milk for her usual cereal.

"I know. We've both got busy days tomorrow," he responded. "How's Veronica?"

Jennifer brightened at the question. "Surgery went well." She was glad now that it had been pushed back twice. The surgeons had needed an extra two hours to deal with what they found when removing the mass. Veronica would not have been strong enough for that if they'd scheduled it sooner. "She mentioned you stopped by the recovery room. She thinks you look cute in the surgical scrubs and booties."

"Most females do."

She cocked her head, laughed, and tossed her pillow at him.

He settled it behind him. "I like Veronica. And the surgeons did a good job. I think she'll heal fine without any need for reconstructive work. She's got a lot of courage, facing a disease that's so unpredictable in how and when it will strike."

"Her mom is struggling with the situation more than Veronica is, I think."

"Understandable."

Tom pointed at a brighter star in the sky. "I'm probably wrong, but I think that's Jupiter, hanging low below that triangle of bright stars."

"I know the Big Dipper and the Milky Way arm. Other than that, they're just stars."

"God has them all named."

"You think so?"

"Hm-mm."

"The alphabet He used must have more than twenty-six letters in it."

Tom smiled. "Probably." He looked over at her. "How about coming to church with me Sunday, maybe go out to lunch afterward? We eventually need to do something planned rather than just take walks when it fits the end of a day."

"I don't go to church, Tom."

His look turned curious. "Why not?"

"I just don't."

"Would you like to give it a try? I go to a Christian church over on Beech Street, just across from the eye clinic. You could come with me Sunday and see what you think."

The idea of going to church with him held zero appeal. She hesitated a beat too long in her search to find a way of politely saying no, and he must have taken the silence as a maybe.

"It's not that intimidating a place," he reassured her. "They have decent coffee, songs with the words provided; the pastor's messages this month are from the book of Luke. You won't have to give money, or feel like you'll be introduced to people, or brace to be asked awkward questions. People are friendly enough. And I'd be there to make sure . . ."

She was laughing. "Okay. I get the point. It's not quite as bad as a visit to the dentist. But you're over-playing it a bit, I think."

"Yeah, I probably am. But I really would like you to come."

She felt trapped in a way she hadn't felt for a very long time. *Church.* He probably didn't even consider the whole thing a big deal. It was for him just church with lower-case emphasis, while for her it pretty much was an all-capitals word. "Since I'll be dressed up for the occasion, we could have lunch somewhere afterward?"

"Yes."

She bit her lip, but decided from his perspective the invitation really wasn't a big deal and overreacting to it just said more about herself than she would like. "I'm on call this Sunday."

"You won't be the only doctor there with a pager on. If you get called in, I'll bring you over to the hospital and hang around until you're done."

"Okay. This is just to see what I think," she said, feeling like she needed to add something to temper her agreement.

"Thanks."

"I get to decide how we spend the afternoon."

He smiled. "Now, that could be dangerous. What do you have in mind?"

She considered it. "Shopping."

He grimaced but gamely nodded. "Just so long as you don't spread the word around the hospital that that was how we spent the afternoon."

"If the past is any clue to how I am around stores, you'll be carrying a lot of sacks before I'm done. I don't get to shop very often, so I make the most of it."

"I appreciate the warning." He finished his drink. "Want a refill?"

"Please."

He disappeared back inside and soon returned with their glasses. "Seriously, you'll like church, and I'll like introducing you to some of my friends. All you've basically seen so far is the doctor side of my life, and there's more than just that on occasion."

"I suspected as much. What time are you going to pick me up?"

"Say nine thirty, and we'll go to the second service."

She nodded, silently hoping there would be a non-critical page about nine ten Sunday morning, so she'd have an excuse to miss the service. How could she explain that church felt scary to her, as if she were in deep waters she didn't understand?

Jennifer walked across the parking lot with Tom, relieved the church service was over.

He unlocked the car door and held it open for her. "Is there anything particular you'd love to have for lunch?"

"Chinese, if you don't mind." She slid into the car seat, careful of her dress and the high heels she didn't wear that often.

"I know a great place," he promised as he settled behind the wheel. The church parking lot was nearly full, with most people leaving at the same time. He let the car idle while other vehicles pulled out. "You were a good sport to come. What did you think?"

"People were friendly enough, and at least it wasn't a service where part of it was in Latin."

He smiled. "It wasn't what you were expecting."

"I don't know that I had an expectation. I just . . . well, I won't say I was lost, but in some ways it was like attending a medical seminar in something not my specialty. I understood the words, but not what was being said. I still don't understand what you believe or why."

He looked over at her. "What would you like to ask?"

"I don't know—that's part of the problem. Maybe I could borrow your Bible? I guess I've never read it before." She didn't want to extend this conversation further. She wasn't that curious, but she felt like it was the only appropriate answer at this point. Tom had brought the book with him from home, and when the pastor started reading, Tom shared his so she could read along too.

"Sure." He'd placed it on the back seat, and he reached around to pick it up. He offered the book to her.

It had thin paper pages, and the text was laid out in two columns like newsprint. "Where do I start?" she asked rather tentatively. If he said to start at the beginning, she would be reading for a year or two before getting to the page they'd read that morning.

"Here." Tom opened the Bible in her hands to where he'd put his handout for the order of service. "This side of the page is what the pastor was reading. If you back up about ten pages—" he showed her— "you'll be at the start of the book of Luke. Why don't you start reading from there?

"I like Luke," Tom went on, "because he was a doctor, and he writes with a doctor's attention to detail about what he saw and heard regarding Jesus. Luke talks about Jesus' birth and childhood and the public ministry He began when He was thirty. The entire book is only about fifty pages, and if you read it, you'll have a pretty good idea of what I believe and why. It isn't intended to be obscure or hard to understand."

"Are you sure you don't mind loaning this to me?"

"I've got several Bibles—it's not a problem."

She slid the program back in the page to note where Luke began. "I'll read and see what I think. And I'll take good care of your Bible. I can tell you use this one a lot." The pages were marked with passages underlined, and notes scrawled in the margins.

"Jen . . ." He waited until she looked at him. "It's okay to tell me after you read Luke that you still don't get it or that it seems strange to believe it's true. Faith has to be something that is reasoned and thought about; otherwise, it's just going along with the crowd. And that's not going to mean much, either to yourself or to God."

"You'll be disappointed if I say I don't get it."

"Disappointed, but still hopeful. I wrestled with the whole question of faith for several years before I chose to believe what the Bible says is true." He smiled. "I'm not holding this up as something you have to pass or fail. What kind of friend would that be? I'd just like you to be curious about God. Read Luke and tell me what you think. That would be a good place to start."

"Okay." She put the book with her purse.

He joined the stream of cars flowing toward the street exit. "Chinese for lunch, then shopping, as promised. Do you have an idea where you want to begin?"

"I need a new pair of dress shoes, so a shoe store, or three or four of them. I'm choosy about shoes."

"Better than I could have hoped for—at least there will be a place I can sit down."

She laughed. "There is that. Then I need a new outfit for the Fourth of July family gathering. It's a big deal."

"Dress up?"

"Opposite. Think downscale—way down. The most obnoxious T-shirt I can find. I may be pitching the family softball game. They have to be distracted enough to not see the pitch coming."

"Got it. Do me a favor and take pictures at this gathering. I already like your family and I've never even met them."

"I plan to. I love pictures."

"I've noticed. And just to be forewarned—I'm going to get a shot of the two of us before the end of this day, even if we have to cram into one of those mall photo booths."

"I'm game," Jennifer agreed, laughing. She had several snapshots of him from the kids' party now tucked in her billfold, but none of the two of them together yet. She'd like to have that photo, regardless of what their future held.

This was the kind of spring she had always enjoyed, one filled with new opportunities and wonderings about what might be coming next. She wanted it captured in photos. She wanted to dream a bit about what might be.

5

Dawn was just barely lightening the sky as Jennifer pulled a chair up to a hospital bedside in a sixth-floor private room. One look at the medevac flight roster from overnight and the list of who had been admitted, and her plans for the day had changed.

"Hi, Kelly."

The girl stirred, turned her head, and joy lit her eyes. "Hi, Doc."

She was pale and thin and looked so much older than her age. Already she was three years past the last birthday her doctors thought she would ever see. Jennifer laid the book she'd wrapped on the blanket so the girl could easily reach it. "Happy birthday," she said softly.

Kelly smiled. "Thanks. I told you I'd make it to twelve."

"Yes, you did, my brave girl. I'm so proud of you."

Kelly's lungs were filling, every breath was a struggle, and in a matter of hours she would be back in the ICU. She'd long ago moved on to more specialized care than this hospital and its medical professionals could provide her. Because Creggle's Syndrome was so rare, only a few physicians in the country had the experience to help Kelly. But whenever the end arrived, the family had known it might be this way—a bad cold turning into pneumonia, and a flight to the nearest hospital equipped to keep her breathing.

"I'm sorry your vacation ended this way," Jennifer said, hurting to see her young friend struggling. She leaned over to recheck the IV line and took hold of the child's hands to determine how chilled she was, even with the fever.

"I got to see the Lincoln Memorial," Kelly whispered, smiling again. "I always wanted to stand there and look at that really big sculpture. I'd thought I might sit on his lap, but it was too high." They both chuckled, then Kelly added, "We did the White House tour. I don't know how Dad arranged it, but he did."

"I'm glad." Jennifer really was glad, but she felt her smile was a bit shaky. The girl had talked about the trip for years, researching every facet of the stops and what they could see. She'd been in good health before the trip—as prepared as the medical community could make her for what had been a lifelong dream. No one wanted to deny her the one thing she most wanted in her life while she still had the ability to enjoy it.

"Don't be sad, Doc," Kelly whispered. "We've licked colds before. I will again."

"I know." Jennifer squeezed her hand. "Do you want me to read to you for a while from your birthday book?"

Kelly nodded.

"I found a copy of my favorite story for you."

"Miss Mandy?" Kelly asked, her voice sounding thrilled despite being weak.

"I found it in a very old box of my treasured books," Jennifer replied, grateful she'd spent the hours searching in the hope it had been saved. She opened the birthday wrappings and showed Kelly the find. Over thirty years old, the book had seen much better days, but the story was still a treasured one. "It's now autographed to you."

She'd told Kelly the story many times from memory as they walked together around hospital halls, Kelly trying to do one more lap and Jennifer encouraging her on.

"Read me the wedding scene with the dog and cat and the cake."

"A perfect place to drop into the story." Jennifer nodded as she found the page. She hoped her memory of the story would come close to what the book would now actually portray.

Jennifer found the box of coffee filters and pushed around cans in her cupboard to find the decaf. She normally drank tea this late at night, but Tom had never acquired the taste for it.

It had been difficult to smile today as she saw the rest of her patients, hard to pass on the normal optimism she could bring to even the toughest situations. The sadness tonight was heavy enough she was glad Tom had offered to stay a few minutes after bringing her home.

He leaned against the counter beside her while she set up the coffee maker. "You haven't told your family about me yet, have you?"

She glanced over and saw the photo he held. She found the energy to smile, took the picture of the

Dee Henderson

O'Malleys from his hand and put it back under the magnet on her refrigerator. "It's not that I don't want to. There just hasn't been the appropriate time. I announce you without some groundwork being laid first, and a couple days later you'll have a U.S. Marshal walking through your office door to give you the third degree."

"I survived medical school and then a surgical residency. Your brothers aren't going to intimidate me."

"Okay, then it will be my sister Lisa, the forensic pathologist, walking through your office door, demanding your life story."

"I'll give you that one. Lisa would be a challenge." He smiled. "Face it, Jennifer. You've got an interesting family. I'd like to meet them one day."

He was comfortable in his authority as a surgeon and good at handling the unexpected, but she knew he still had no real concept of what it would be like to meet the O'Malleys. This wasn't a simple equation, and she didn't know how to explain why; she just knew it inside and wasn't going to take a risk yet. "I really do want you to meet them. And we'll talk about it."

"Rachel seems nice."

"They are all nice. They're just . . . protective. I'm the youngest, and they consider themselves all rather invested in what's going on in my life. I can't rush words like *boyfriend* into their vocabulary."

Tom settled his arms around her waist and rested his chin on her shoulder. "I like that word."

The hug was smoothly done, comforting, and for one brief moment she closed her eyes just to snapshot the emotions and tuck them away to savor later. She smiled. "We'll get you and my family together, but it's not something I plan to rush into."

"As long as it's only me on your list." He hugged her a last moment, then stepped away. "Coffee, then I'll head home. Where's that burned-out light bulb you wanted me to look at?"

"Back hallway by the garage. Replacements are in the utility room."

"One tall man to the rescue."

She laughed. "I think one short girl with a chair could do it just fine too. I just haven't had time."

"Lack of height, lack of time—what's the difference? It got you to laugh." Whistling, he headed off toward the utility room.

She poured water into the coffee maker. "I do appreciate the laughter," she whispered, glad he was there. Work tomorrow would be heavy, and this time with him had given her the space she'd needed to breathe. It was a small thing, but she was now letting the emotions and burdens of her responsibilities, sometimes life-and-death ones, flow over and rest on his shoulders when the days were markedly hard. She hadn't told him about Kelly—some things were too close to tears to talk about—but he'd probably guessed.

Tom left for home a half hour later, and Jennifer wisely began preparing for bed rather than work another hour on paperwork as she often did before turning in.

She sat on the bed and picked up the photo on the bedside table. It was a more informal picture of the O'Malleys than the one Tom had seen on the refrigerator. She had been the last one chosen, the last selected to be an O'Malley, and she'd spent the final years at Trevor House more than blessed by the group's decision to invite her to be one of them. They had survived by thriving together, and it mattered so very much what her family thought of Tom.

They would like him because she cared about him. She didn't question that. But beyond that she wanted them to personally think he was a great guy, and she knew that kind of respect would have to be earned with time. She wanted the family to get to know Tom in the ways she had. To appreciate his humor. To appreciate his heart. To trust him. So she hesitated to mention him. Not because it mattered so little, but because it mattered so much.

She'd have to figure out a way to tell them about Tom over the Fourth of July gathering. Low-key, casual, but clear enough they would understand he might one day be more than just a good friend.

That thought was enough to make her hesitate even more. She hadn't been looking for a guy to appear in her life, and now that he had, she was still not entirely sure where she wanted the relationship to go.

He had so many parts of his life beyond work that she was just beginning to find out about, church being one of the larger ones. She still hadn't met his family either, and she knew they were as important to him as the O'Malleys were to her.

She put the photo back on the table. She'd figure it out.

She set her alarm for five a.m. so she could see Kelly in ICU before her workday began, then turned off the lights.

"What are you watching?"

Jennifer stirred on the couch and looked over to see Tom walking into the playroom of the hospital pediatrics wing. He'd changed from scrubs to street clothes, but the white coat and the notepad he carried said he'd still been finishing his evening rounds. She glanced back at the television and the DVD playing. "A Herbie movie—not sure which one. The kids were watching it earlier."

"I heard the news." He sat down in a chair near her.

She appreciated the understatement and simply nodded her acknowledgment. Kelly Brousher had died, succumbing to heart failure at 7:18 p.m. *Twelve years old.*

Jennifer felt numb.

Tom didn't say anything else, simply sat and watched the movie with her. It was odd, the fact she could watch the movie, appreciate the laughter in its soundtrack, and yet not find the ability to even smile at the funny scenes.

There were charts to update, tomorrow's schedule to review, and she should get some sleep . . . but she didn't move. The pediatrics playroom wasn't the most comfortable place to relax, but it was quiet and uninterrupted at this time of night, and she didn't have to face driving herself home or pretend she was a professional and composed doctor as she passed staff in the halls. She'd finished the intake paperwork for the second of her new cancer patients, seen Wendy settled in, and come down here to collapse for a while.

She was glad for Tom's silence.

The movie was at the scene of the car race along dirt roads, and she watched it just to keep her eyes focused and not filling with tears. "Do you believe in heaven?" She knew he also had days like this one. Surgeons lost patients. It was a simple fact of the world in which they had chosen to work. But she hadn't known she was going to ask the question until it popped out of her mouth. The topic had been pushing at her all evening, demanding to be answered somehow.

"I do."

She looked over, surprised at the confidence she heard in his words.

"An actual heaven, not just a nice concept?"

"Yes."

She hugged the pillow she held in front of her a bit tighter. She wasn't sure what she believed. She just couldn't reconcile the idea the girl who had passed away today was simply gone. Life should be more than that. "Kelly had Creggle's Syndrome, showing on both genes' markers. She never should have lived past six, but she made it to twelve. It wasn't like I didn't know this day was coming. But it's the fact it was pneumonia—something we know how to treat— that we knew to watch for—that makes this so hard to accept. We just couldn't turn it in time."

"I'm so sorry, Jennifer."

"So am I."

She let the couch absorb more of her weight, winced, and shifted to find a more comfortable position for her back. She preferred not to think about the last hours—she'd do enough of that in her dreams tonight. She tipped her right foot and studied the knotted laces. She needed new tennis shoes, she thought idly. These were showing their wear. Her walks with Tom were occasionally making her back hurt hours later—probably the worn-out shoes.

"Have you had dinner yet?"

She shook her head.

"It's almost ten. Come on, I'll buy you a sandwich, and we'll take a moseying kind of walk with no destination. That works for days like this."

"Thanks, but I'll pass this time." She wanted to sit here until the movie finished, then gather together her things and go home to cry in private. She'd been too numb to cry yet, and too smart to let herself go home until more time had flowed by. Kelly had been more than a patient over the last six years. She'd been a friend. Jennifer knew that when she started crying, it wasn't going to be pretty or soon over.

Tom stood and held out his hand. "Grieving alone

is an absolute waste of good emotions. Come on. You're going to eat and walk."

She let him pull her to her feet. "Sometimes I regret being a doctor."

He settled his arm across her shoulders. "Only on nights your heart gets broken."

Deep in her heart she knew he was right, but she shook her head.

"Tomorrow will be a new day," he reassured her. "The hurt gets less."

"That's what I'm afraid of, that I'll forget her," she whispered.

"You never forget the patients that touch your heart. And there are a number of photos on your refrigerator of the two of you together. Those moments will eventually be what you remember more than today."

"I don't think I'm cut out for this, Tom." The hole in her heart tonight simply ached. Every child she opened her heart to risked becoming a loss like this.

"No one is." He turned her toward the hall. She reached up to grasp his hand, glad he'd come to find her.

"I thought we might go to a ball game this week," she offered, "if you're interested. There were tickets floating around the office today for a game Wednesday night."

"I'm interested. I like the fact you just offered to schedule something on both our calendars."

"I just hate to plan something and get disappointed when it doesn't work out. You know one of us is likely to get paged away."

"Probably. We'll just reschedule for another game if it does."

Tom seemed to understand her need to find some way out of the grief she was experiencing, and he turned the conversation to games he'd seen with his father through the years. It was the sound of his voice that was comforting, and Jennifer tucked away that knowledge to think about later as she walked along beside him and listened.

The ball game Wednesday evening was a successful outing, both as a date and because their team won. The same for the show Tom bought tickets for a week later, and Jennifer decided to stop wondering where the friendship might be headed and simply enjoy it.

That he was trying to lighten the complex relationship she had with her work, help her sort out the emotions of Kelly's passing, while fully supporting the love she showered on her kids began to settle in as something unique she'd never before experienced. Tom wasn't attempting to get her to split work away from the rest of her life and build in distance. He was working instead to make it possible for her to cope with what happened, to care deeply but still have a life that could exist alongside the job.

She was aware their friendship was moving beyond friends to something more, but it was flowing forward in such a measured way she wasn't feeling either pressured or rushed, just cared for, and cared about.

For the first time she was beginning to wonder what might be possible if the relationship lasted through the summer or beyond. The very idea of being fully settled in life had seemed like an unattainable dream only months before, and now it seemed almost possible.

"What do you think about this one?" She held up a T-shirt she'd found. She was still searching for what she would take with her to Chicago for the O'Malley July gathering, and they were wandering Dallas's open-air market to explore more options. "Purple and green clashed when I was growing up, but it doesn't seem like any colors clash anymore."

Tom tipped his head as he considered it. "You would look about twelve. But cute."

She thought about that and tucked the shirt under her arm. "That's a good fact. I'm feeling old lately.

Gregory asked if I was going to be as old as his grand-
mother someday."

"What did you say?"

"That I would be, but only after he was married and
had kids of his own. He told me he thinks it will be a
long time, as he doesn't like girls, and he first wants
to ride horses like that leaning cowboy in the mural."

"The mere idea of Gregory on a horse from which
he could fall is enough to make me shudder."

"I know. Maybe ten years from now I'll stop worrying about him breaking any more bones."

Tom came over and perched a straw hat, its brim
circled with colorful ribbons, on her head. "This
works. You need more sun protection when we go
wandering about. And you can wear it at your Fourth
celebration."

She considered the display of hats where he'd selected it. "Going to buy yourself one too?"

"You can pick it out for me. I'll trust you."

She put the hat on top of her stack of purchases
and handed them over to him. "Go check out for me,
and I'll find you the perfect one."

He obligingly took the items and her cash. "How
are we doing on time?"

She glanced at her watch. "Another hour."

They were going to dinner with two of the partners

in his practice, and after that to a movie. She'd agreed to go to church tomorrow with him, and if both their pagers cooperated, they would be working on hanging pictures in his house tomorrow afternoon. The weekend was filling up the way she hoped many more would in the future—little things that created memories.

She found the perfect cowboy hat for Tom. She took it over to him and tugged him down a bit so that she could put it on his head. "Very nice."

"I was afraid you'd get me one with ribbons."

"I'm kinder than that most of the time." She accepted the stuffed bag he handed her and waited while he bought the hat. "You know what? You're starting to enjoy shopping."

He smiled. "Or maybe I'm just enjoying watching you."

6

"Thanks for talking about this and not pushing. I like going to church with you. I just don't understand much of this yet." Jennifer shifted the books she carried as she and Tom walked along a park path where they had retreated from the Sunday-evening crowds. It was important to him, church, and she was trying her best to understand why.

She'd read the book of Luke as a favor to him, and read other parts of the Bible in smaller sections, but it was hard to make sense of all the information that flowed at her—about God, about Israel's history, about Jesus, about the church.

"What else can I answer for you?"

"How do you *know*, Tom? That the Bible, that Christianity, is true?"

"I wish I had a brilliant answer for you. I guess, as with most things, you start with common sense." Tom walked a bit, then bent to pick up a small branch on the path. He snapped the wood in two pieces and held them up.

"The Bible tells about how people would take a piece of wood, use part of it to start a fire, and use the other part to carve out an image of a god, then worship that image and pray to it for rain and good fortune. As if the works of their own hands could come alive and answer them. It's illogical and foolish. So common sense will knock down most religions." He tossed aside the sticks.

"Other religions sound good on the surface, but turn out to be impersonal systems based on grading what you *do* to determine your worth. Christianity is the only religion that promises not a system but a personal God you have a relationship with. At its core, Christianity is a relationship with a God who is listening, responding, and interacting with those who love Him. That's how you prove it, Jen. You test

Christianity's claims by testing out the relationship on which it's built."

"Can you have a relationship with God if you don't believe in Him?" she asked. "That doesn't seem possible. Isn't Christianity something you have to take on faith first? Jesus is the Son of God. Jesus died for people's sins. Jesus rose from the dead. Those are hard facts to absorb and believe."

Tom weighed her question, then nodded. "Consider it this way. If you step off a tall building, it's immaterial whether you think gravity is true or not; it's still going to splat you on the ground a few seconds later. Right?"

"Thanks for *that* image."

He smiled. "It got the point across. In some ways it doesn't matter what you believe. Christianity is more like that gravity analogy than not. God is God right now, and He will still be God tomorrow, regardless of whether you choose to believe in Him today or not. That's a good thing. It means you can ask questions and search out answers and see for yourself what is true. God will still go on being God while you ponder the questions. He doesn't mind."

He nodded toward the books she carried. "So read the Bible. Test it. Does God do what He says He will do? Is God behaving as He said He would? And if what you read and see does seem to be consistent, then maybe you might start by praying something like, 'God, if you are really there, I want to get to know you so I can believe in you too.' If Christianity is real, you're going to find there's a very personal God waiting to respond to you and help with the questions you have."

She didn't understand how interacting with God was supposed to work, but she found it hard to put that question into words without sounding foolish.

"You can quit biting that lip, Jen," he said, smiling and slowing their walk to a stop. "God loves you. He's not going to hide the evidence and the answers to the questions you wonder about. He's going to help your search lead to answers. God says that those who seek Him will find Him. I'm not afraid to say check it out and see. You'll find Christianity is true."

"What about the things that simply can't be proved? Jesus is the Son of God. Jesus died for our sins. Jesus rose from the dead. It's hard to prove something like the resurrection."

"What happened two thousand years ago can be studied, Jen. You can't see gravity, but you can see lots of evidence that gravity exists. You can find a lot of evidence that the resurrection actually happened. Both the record for the crucifixion and resurrection stand up to intense scrutiny."

He tapped the copy of C. S. Lewis's *Mere Christianity* he'd pulled off his shelf for her. They started walking again. "This one is good for some more information to mull over. Nearly everyone will acknowledge there was a man named Jesus who lived two thousand years ago in the land of Palestine. The Roman historians of the time, the archaeological record—it's not hard to find the evidence of Jesus that comes from numerous sources other than the Bible. The debate is about who that man was. A good teacher? A religious prophet? Or what He claimed to be—the Son of God."

Jennifer nodded. "I'll concede to you that if you're right, then I'd be foolish not to at least weigh the evidence. But, Tom, don't you really want me to believe more because *you* believe than anything else?"

"I admit it's hard, sharing so much of my life with you but knowing this part that is so important to me is kind of a black hole for you. I find myself not talking about subjects I would normally mention because I know we don't share the same perspective yet." He stopped and reached over a hand to rest on hers. "I'm sorry I'm not more eloquent at explaining things for you."

"It's more clarity than I've had before," she offered. "I've gone a lifetime without being asked to consider Christianity. If you hadn't come along, I probably wouldn't be doing so now. But I care about what matters to you. I want to understand it. I just can't promise I'll believe like you do."

"I know that, Jen. I'm only asking that you consider it." Tom smiled. "God's not asking you to deserve or earn the fact He loves you. He's not asking you to do something to be worthy of being loved. He just loves you. Jesus paid the full price of your sins so you can be with Him for eternity. That really is how simple Christianity is. A personal God who loves you, wants a relationship with you, and who has been willing to go to extraordinary lengths to make that possible. He'll do most of the heavy lifting to help you figure this out. You simply have to be willing to give Him a chance."

She hesitated, then asked one further question that had been bothering her. "Why should I matter to Him? I'm just one person, and God—if He exists as you describe—is so much more."

"Your worth is measured by how He sees you, not by something you have done or could do in the future. It's okay to trust that. You matter because God says you do."

"All I can promise is that I'll think about it."

"That's all I'm asking," Tom assured her.

Tom trailed Jennifer into her office, grateful there had been a break penciled into her day's schedule in an overflow slot. Their calendars had finally clicked for him to join her for a Monday. "I forgot how absolutely draining it is to see a string of patients, one right after the other."

Jennifer laughed and pointed him toward her desk chair. "You looked like you were beginning to wilt a couple of times. Sit. Dig out that lunch you brought and never ate. I've got some files to pull for the rest of my patients this afternoon."

He turned her desk chair around and settled in. He worked hard as a surgeon, but it was a much more controlled, absorbed kind of focus. He'd complete a complex surgery and look up to find six hours had passed, feeling the exhaustion when the patient was moved safely into the recovery room. But for the most part, during the surgery he was unaware of it. Jennifer had days where ten minutes being focused on one thing was a long stretch of time.

He opened a soda. "How do you keep the kids straight? So far today, among others, there was a Kim, Kathy, and Karen, not to mention three Mikes."

Jennifer thumbed through files in her credenza, pulling out an occasional name. She smiled at the question. "Kim wants to be a ballerina, Kathy is a budding scientist, and Karen has blond hair and likes boys and wants to be in the movies someday. They are as different as kids can be."

She glanced over her shoulder. "And the Mikes—don't get me started. One is so shy he will barely look at me, despite the fact he often calls the office to ask my opinion about what his cancer doctor told him. The oldest Mike hates taking pills and thinks doctors are a waste of his time but comes because the pain in his leg is too bad to not admit it hurts. And the youngest Mike is an animal lover—there was an actual breathing frog in his pocket at the last visit."

She pulled another file. "I could give you the symptoms they came in with if that would help you sort them out, but symptoms tend to change with visits, so I just remember the kids." She found the last file she needed and pushed the credenza closed.

"You do understand most doctors don't rattle off particulars that easily." He broke his sandwich in half and passed her part of it. "Not when they have over a hundred patients."

"It's that many?" she said around a bite.

"I asked your chief nurse."

Jennifer shook her head. "I see them one at a time. It's not that big a deal to remember a few details."

"Jennifer, that hundred number was just the last

month. You're here or at the hospital most of the time. You basically see kids from the time you arrive to the time you finally call it a night. You need another partner here in your practice."

"I need a new pair of tennis shoes," she said. She held up the sandwich. "This is pretty good. What's on it?"

"Ham and bologna, I think, with some kind of smoked cheese. Whatever was left in my fridge that still smelled edible." He opened a bag of chips. "Change of subject. What about July Fourth?"

"What about it?"

"To meet your family. I can get some time off. You said your family is already planning to get together that weekend."

"You'd really consider coming to Chicago with me?"

"Sure."

She bit her lip.

He laughed. "It's not going to ruin our friendship, Jen. Even if they don't like me at all, they'll still be in Chicago, and I'll still be the one dropping by your office every day or so. Our relationship can handle me meeting your family, and them meeting me."

"I just . . . we're not your everyday family, Tom. I need you to understand that going in. We're all closer than most because we've had to be."

"You worry too much. They'll like me. Just think about it, okay?"

"Sure, I'll think about it." She looked at the chips. "Got extras of those?" she asked.

He pushed over the bag. "I brought two bags. So if we see patients until six, as this schedule seems to suggest, we'd better plan dinner now because I'm going to be totally wiped by the end of the day."

"My place," she offered. "I think I can find enough for a stir-fry if you want to play chef and put it together while I make a salad."

"I'm game." He ran his finger along her calendar. "Ricky is next?"

"Ten. Wants to be a firefighter. Loves adventure. Has bone cancer that refuses to be checked." She picked up the boy's file and passed it over.

"Talk to me about his oncologist. Who does he see?"

She settled on the corner of her desk and worked on the bag of chips. "Dr. Shayfield. They've already tried the standard protocols." Tom flipped pages in the chart while she started running down drugs and dates from memory, adding commentary on how Ricky had responded.

He had thought he was skilled as a surgeon, but he'd realized today after about the sixth patient that he was working with a general practice MD who knew more about caring for patients than he'd learned so far in his whole career. If she didn't have a photographic memory for the details of this job, she had a focus on her kids that made her memory rock solid.

"The goal right now is to keep the pain in check," she added, "deal with two biopsy incisions that are refusing to fully heal, and figure out how to keep his spirits up. He's seeing oncologists every week now, and he's getting discouraged."

"Got some ideas?"

"Nope. But I'll listen to him until I hear something I can work with." She shrugged. "All that medical school and I'm back to what my mom would have recommended. General practice is pretty far from the certainty of surgery."

"I'm remembering." He finished his apple and threw away the remnants of lunch. "Let's go see Ricky. Who brings him in?"

"Normally his mom." Jennifer pushed open the office door and headed toward the nurses' station to get the sign-in chart. Tom followed, glad he had made these arrangements so he could step into her world and see what she did during a workday. He was getting an education on what it was like to be a top-tier general-practice doctor. If he hadn't seen this day for himself, he never would have understood what she meant when she occasionally commented it had been a busy day.

7

Jennifer stretched out in the warmth of the sun, a stack of books beside her deck chair. It was easier to read these while at Tom's than carry the books back and forth to her home. She could hear Tom still on the phone inside, talking about a surgery scheduled for the following Monday. When he was finished with his call, he was going to take her shopping, and she thought she would enjoy this day more than most.

She picked up his Bible. She didn't mind the studying Tom was asking of her. This was important to him, and it required some of her time, but he wasn't pushy about it or insisting she put blind faith in something she didn't understand.

She did see consistency in him and in what the Bible said was true about Christians. He was a surgeon, at peace with life. That came from somewhere. The highs and lows that seemed to pace her own life didn't seem to be his experience. He lost patients, but it didn't bury him in sadness. He had hope in something after this life, and it changed how he viewed the events that happened to him and around him. She was beginning to appreciate how powerful an advantage that gave him when trouble came.

"What are you reading?"

She turned the Bible so Tom could see the page. "Luke. Where I started reading the Bible all those weeks ago. The book makes more sense now."

"Does it?"

"It reads less theoretical, more factual. I read about Jesus healing someone who was blind and it no longer jars as impossible to believe. If Jesus is God, as He says He is, healing a blind man should have been as simple a task as Luke describes. There's no need to make a big production out of making a blind man see when you have the power to create sight to begin with. It would seem more out of place if Jesus had made a big deal out of it."

"I'm glad it's starting to ring true."

"At least I'm beginning to understand why you believe Jesus is God, even if I still have a lot of questions about the implications of what that claim means." She closed the book and set it on the stack beside her. "How are things at the hospital?"

"We're ready for Monday."

"Good." She pulled on her shoes. "I'm ready to go if you are."

"How on earth did I let you talk me into shopping again?"

She grinned and caught his hand. "Face it, you *like* shopping with me."

"Do you have a list this time?"

"I do."

"We'll do this efficiently then."

She laughed. "You can only hope."

They headed toward the mall parking lot, crowded with shoppers coming and going. Tom unlocked the car and opened the trunk. Jennifer added another two packages to her accumulated pile. "That's the last item on the list. I'm done. For now."

Tom rested an arm around her shoulders. "I like you, Jennifer."

She glanced up at him and laughed. "I'm starting to really like you too."

"Tell you what then, little shrimp, I think we should go do something a lot more fun to fill up the rest of the afternoon."

"Little shrimp?" she asked, wondering where the teasing was coming from, but letting him get away with it. "What do you have in mind?"

"I'm shopped out, walked out . . . and movies are a nice place to hold your hand but not much for conversation. What do you say we go play golf or something like that?"

"I've never played golf."

"Never? As in not ever, never, none?" He turned her toward the passenger-side door. "This we have to fix."

"I'm pretty good at miniature golf."

He winced. "That is definitely not the mental image I have in mind for our golfing future. We'll start at the driving range. Buckets and buckets of golf balls, and a nice single driver that will let you smack those balls for two hundred yards without blinking. We can work on your putt and actually getting a ball into a small hole sometime later."

Jennifer hit the golf ball and watched it soar, hoping to hit the big target straight ahead of her that read *200 yards*. She missed.

"That's better," Tom encouraged, smiling. "It only sliced into the next county."

Jennifer wrinkled her nose at him. That golf ball had sailed left with great purpose. "Maybe by the time I get to the bottom of this bucket, that will be fixed. Maybe I just need a better teacher."

"It's going exactly where you told it to go. Look at where you want it to go, look down at the ball, and swing. Don't turn your head as you hit the ball to see where you want it to go. Just smack the daylights out of the thing."

She laughed and positioned another golf ball on the plastic tee. "You make this sound so easy, and it's anything but simple." She settled back into position for a swing and checked her grip on the driver. "The next one is going to be solid."

It sliced left again. "Shoot."

Tom laughed.

She found herself more amused by the minute with the fact he'd talked her into trying this. She pointed the club at him. "Five more tries, then I'm admitting defeat. And you will be too."

She got out another golf ball, took two test swings with the club, and clenched her teeth at the pain in her back before the second swing was done. She lowered the club to the ground to brace herself and gingerly took a step away from the grass square.

Tom had hold of her elbows to steady her before she got the second step taken. "How bad?" He didn't have to ask what had happened; he'd have seen her expression change as her back muscles tightened up.

"Just a pulled muscle that's not holding its own." She was glad he was supporting her. Her left leg had just gone numb again.

"You're seeing a doctor, one that's good at back injuries."

She blew out a breath. "Right now I'll settle for sitting down."

He guided her over to a nearby bench. "I didn't even think—"

"Don't, Tom. I've been fine the last month. I never thought about it either." She sat down and carefully shifted her position until the pain in her back seemed to fade away. "Relax, it's already beginning to wear off. Why don't you go find me a soda? I'll take a couple Tylenol, and while they kick in, I'll sit here and watch you show me how a pro would swing that golf club."

"Others here can use the bucket of golf balls. I'm taking you home to get an ice pack."

"Start with the soda, and we'll see," she compromised. It wasn't the end of the world—she'd just aggravated a pulled muscle that had apparently never fully healed.

Monday morning Jennifer chose to sit on the edge of the exam table with her feet propped up on a chair. She wasn't interested in being a patient, but given Tom's insistence, she didn't have much choice. She'd taken a great deal of care in choosing her personal doctor, and today that fact was going to matter.

The door swung open and a lady small in stature but big in heart came into the exam room, a group of medical students trailing in her wake. She sent them on their way with a wave of her hand. "My office in twenty minutes, students. Find some notes to write." They obediently flowed back out.

Tina Landers turned, studied Jennifer's face, and sat down on the stool beside her. "What's been going on, Jennifer? I saw the notation on Heather's schedule for me today."

Jennifer liked that Tina didn't even think about picking up and reading the chart her nurse had meticulously filled out. Instead she went right to the heart of the matter.

"I picked up a three-year-old several weeks ago, and it must have been at an odd angle. I pulled something in my back. It's never really gone away but rather seems to flare up at the most inconvenient times. I think I might have a disk slipping out of place."

"Sharp pain when it comes?"

"More like weakness. My back just suddenly gives out and refuses to let me pick something or someone up. Or my leg goes numb. The pain is more like an ongoing ache with an occasional breathtaking stab."

"I'd ask if you get much exercise to keep your back limber, but I know your schedule. You walk a marathon around this hospital every week."

"True. But lately I've been going for the elevators rather than the stairs, and that's not like me."

"You voluntarily walking into my office tells me this is more than just occasionally catching you off guard. What are you taking for the pain?"

"Tylenol. Anything else isn't worth the side effects."

"Any other aches and pains going on? Your joints, your muscles?"

"No."

"Any colds, fevers, headaches?"

"Nothing beyond what I catch once in a while from patients."

Her doctor took hold of her hands. "Any coldness, sensations of being light-headed, unusual balance problems?"

Jennifer shook her head.

"Any bruising, tenderness? Have you fallen?"

"No."

"Anything beyond lifting up the boy that seems to coincide with the symptoms?"

"Lifting the boy probably aggravated something that was already there. I've had the occasional back-ache for a couple of years now. I assumed it was the bike riding, so I switched to walking instead. That about made it disappear."

Tina lifted Jennifer's feet one at a time, checking reflexes to touch. She retrieved her stethoscope and listened to the pulse in each ankle. "I hear you've been seeing Tom Peterson."

Jennifer smiled. "Are there any secrets around this hospital?"

"Gina is his chief surgical nurse, and I've been

friends with her forever. He's a nice man, from what I hear."

"He is," Jennifer agreed.

Tina stepped back and slid her stethoscope back into her pocket. "Let's find out what is going on. Can I schedule you for the tests we'll need this week?"

"Maybe later this week to start things? I'm covering for Larry the next few days. And I honestly don't think this is urgent, just persistent."

"Tell you what. I'll write the scripts and you can work the tests in as they fit your schedule. X-ray, MRI, blood work. While I have the chance to get the data, you can have the rest of the physical for free. You're long overdue."

"I'd say thanks, but this is not going to be fun."

"You'll be glad once it's done. Hospital policy for staff—nothing goes through with your name on the tests—so what shall we call you?"

"How about Darla Reese?"

Tina noted it on her prescription pad. "Why don't you bring dinner with you and stop by my office Thursday evening around seven, say two weeks from now? I'll try to clear the backlog of paperwork on Thursdays, so I'll be in. We'll look at the test results and pictures that have come back by then and talk. We'll get this figured out."

Jennifer tucked the list Tina handed her into her pocket. "Thanks, Tina."

The woman smiled and moved toward the door. "Tell Tom I said hi. Call me if anything changes in the meantime."

"I will."

Jennifer was grateful for the slight reprieve. At least she'd be able to tell Tom when he asked that she'd seen her doctor, and if the tests were fit in over the next week or so, maybe he would accept that simple assurance for how she was doing. He watched her more closely than she realized at times, and the last thing she wanted was him worrying about her.

She glanced at her watch and knew she was going to be pushed for time to see all her patients and still get over to the hospital to watch Tom in surgery that afternoon. Instead of continuing to make assumptions, she wanted to return the favor and get a better idea for what his workday was like. But it had never seemed to fit into her day to be there as of yet.

Her pager chirped. She read the text as she left the exam room. Veronica had begun running a fever.

Jennifer pulled a glass serving bowl down from the upper shelf for their salad Wednesday night and moved around Tom at the stove to a work area near the sink. She began shredding lettuce and considered adding some of the spinach he, for some strange reason, actually liked.

"You're awful quiet tonight."

"It was a long day," she replied, choosing to leave it at that. She was looking forward to a meal together, a baseball game on television she could share with him without paying much attention beyond the score, and then an early night.

He leaned into her space. "Coming to meet my parents Thursday?"

She glanced over at him. His attention was focused on the dinner preparations, and she wasn't sure how deliberate the move closer to her had been. "I'm thinking about it."

"You should say yes, you know. Mom makes wonderful lasagna. A whole lot more edible meal than this is going to end up being with me doing the major cooking here."

She smiled. "It's not the food I'm worried about."

"The expectations will be realistic. Mom knows not every girl in town is going to fall in love with her son."

"Hmmm. I think her son has different ideas."

"You can't blame a guy for trying." His arm brushed hers. "I like the new perfume, by the way."

Jennifer nudged him out of her space. Without either of them saying much, she knew they were both aware this had become more than a simple friendship over the last few weeks, but where exactly it was going hadn't really defined itself yet. "Larry said he could take my pager. But I need to be able to come in if Veronica gets worse."

"Not a problem—I'll get you there. How's she doing?"

Jennifer tilted her hand back and forth rather than answer in words. Fever was never a good sign when it showed up in the first weeks after a major surgery. Veronica had the spirit to fight, but her body wasn't cooperating. The fever kept drifting higher and not breaking. "How about if we don't stay too long? Dinner, then come back here?"

Tom smiled. "Now who's nervous? I'll stop by for you at six, we'll have dinner with my folks, and I'll escort you back to your front door by nine. Promise."

"And not a word about maybe being something more than friends someday," she murmured, looking down at the salad to hide her blush.

"I don't think Mom is going to need words to figure it out."

"Promise me anyway."

He reached over and ran a finger along her cheek. "Promise. Trust me."

Trust was something that didn't come particularly easy to any of the O'Malleys, but she knew he was doing his best to make it possible for her to take the next step with him. "Pick me up at six." She was starting to trust this man, and with that was going to come the gift of her heart.

8

Thursday night Tom unlocked the door to Jennifer's home, turned on lights, and stepped inside after her. He opened the hall closet and hung up her jacket for her. She moved into the living room to check for messages on her answering machine. He pushed his hands into his pockets, worried about her. She was still more quiet than normal, had been ever since Veronica's fever had returned. He didn't know how to help. "Thank you for the evening. I know it's not much of a date, spending it with my parents."

She looked back at him with a brief smile. "I loved meeting your parents. It would be so sad if you were living in the same city as them and didn't enjoy spending time together. Your mom and I are going out to lunch sometime next week, and she's bringing her photo albums."

"So I overheard," he noted dryly. He walked over, put an arm around her shoulders, and turned her from the living room toward the kitchen. "Decaf coffee. Then I'm off."

She didn't seem ready to talk about what was going on yet, and pushing it wasn't something that fit the situation, not when sadness seemed to be causing the quietness he sensed in her. "Veronica will be fine," he reassured.

"I hope so."

The hospital halls were quiet at eleven the next evening as Jennifer walked to the room she had visited many times. The page had come shortly after ten. She'd been home, but still up. She tapped on the hospital room door before stepping inside. "Hi, Veronica."

The girl lifted a hand in hello as she tried to smile. Jennifer pulled over a chair and settled in beside her. "How are you doing?"

"Chest hurts tonight," the child whispered.

"There may be a fluid pocket developing where they removed the mass that could be causing some of that," Jennifer said softly, relieved to finally have a medical answer for what was happening.

"They told me. They want to do more surgery."

"Are you okay with that?"

"If it makes me better. Mom is worried. She's talking with the doctors now."

"I know she is. The surgeons are good. They'll be in and out as simply and safely as they can be."

"Will you be there, in the recovery room?"

Jennifer soothed the girl's hand. "I will. And maybe I can get Tom to stop by the recovery room again too."

"He's pretty cool, for a doctor."

"I'll tell him you think so." Jennifer gently squeezed the small hand. "They're going to call folks in and do the surgery tonight, so you don't have to feel so awful for much longer."

"I just want to go home and go back to school and play with my dog . . . normal stuff again. No more hospitals."

"I want that for you too. Let's see if this solves the problem, and then we'll get you sprung from here as fast as we can."

The OR was quiet and orderly and calm. It didn't change the fact everyone there had been called in late on a Friday night because of the urgency with the case. Tom followed Gina to the light board to see the latest pictures, joining Kevin, who was already studying them.

"You know this patient?" Kevin asked.

Tom nodded and examined the film. The fluid pocket was distinct. The X-rays had been clear forty-eight hours before, and no one wanted to wait and see what they would look like in another twelve hours. If this was actually a rupture draining into her chest cavity, every hour was critical.

"A systemic infection not responding to treatment—something is keeping it generated," Kevin remarked. "This looks like the source."

"Let's hope so. If not, opening her up again is going to cause more complications than it solves." Tom scanned the film one last time. The procedure itself would take him only about thirty minutes. They would know soon. "Okay. Let's get this one under way."

Tom leaned against the brick wall, tired from the adrenaline drain even short surgeries always brought. "I think it was the right call," he said to Jennifer, glad she was there but concerned about the fatigue he saw in her face. "There was a smell to the fluid, even though it appeared clear. The lab will have to tell us. The tissue that settled into the void left by the mass looks like it had folded over on itself and may have created a channel for liquids to seep through into the chest cavity. If that was the cause, it's been dealt with, and this shouldn't reoccur."

"Thank you for that good news, Tom."

"You're very welcome."

"I watched you work." She gestured to the glass window. "You look comfortable in there."

"It's my turf."

"More than that. You're sure of yourself and what you're doing."

"I'm comfortable that I know what can be done and how to do it. I just can't always predict the outcome days later. But this time I'll make a reasoned guess that another forty-eight hours of intravenous antibiotics and that fever will break and finally disappear."

He slipped the protective covers off his shoes. "I'm going to get changed. I'll see you in the recovery room shortly. Would you like me to give you a lift home once she's settled? You really need some sleep."

"I think I'll stay awhile and visit with her mom. Thanks for the offer, but go on home."

"Call me when you do get home? Just so I know you didn't fall asleep during the drive."

"I like the fact you worry about me."

"It's getting to be a bad habit, but call me anyway."

"I promise."

Tom watched her head toward the recovery room and knew what his dad meant when he'd remarked after dinner that Jennifer was a giver. Even after she'd given enormous amounts of energy and time, she still had the heart to give more. As a compliment, Tom thought it was one of the best his father could have bestowed.

He rubbed his tired neck and went to change. He wanted the freedom to worry about how much sleep she got, and have the right to do something about it. Instead he'd be going home alone.

Jennifer found comfort just in watching Veronica sleep. The pain, visible this last week on her face even as she slept, was now fading. Her breathing was less labored, and the fever at least checked and not rising.

Jennifer stayed until she was certain the girl would sleep for the rest of the night. After saying good-night to Veronica's mom, she walked to her car and slid into the driver's seat with a sigh. It was a quiet drive home, without much traffic stirring in the still-dark early morning hours.

She arrived home, locked up the house, and walked upstairs. Once in the bedroom, she picked up the phone and dialed a number she knew by heart.

"Hello?"

She'd awakened Tom from a pretty deep sleep, and that made her voice soften even before she spoke. "I'm home. And yes, come to the Fourth of July gathering and meet my family. It will be easier to introduce you in person than to mention you over the phone and have the family grapevine take over and spread the news."

He was quiet for a good half minute. "You won't regret this."

"I hope not."

"Trust me, Jen. You won't regret this." She could tell he was now smiling.

"Good night, Tom. Go back to sleep."

"Yes, ma'am."

She hung up the phone, smiling in return.

Electing to linger at home a few extra minutes before going to the hospital to start weekend rounds, Jennifer called in to check on Veronica, found she'd had a stable night, then fixed herself a bagel and coffee. She brought it into the living room and curled up on the couch. She picked up one of the books on the coffee table.

She'd been thinking last night, before the page about Veronica, about Kelly and what it had been like to lose her. She couldn't help but worry she was going to lose Veronica and face that pain again.

She'd remembered something Kelly had often said in passing. Like Tom, Kelly believed in God, and Jennifer had seen the results of that faith and courage, even on the day Kelly had died. The girl had smiled at the idea of going home to heaven. "'Jesus loves me, this I know . . .'" she'd whispered to explain why she had smiled. Her faith had been real, even as she faced dying.

After a few pages, Jennifer closed Tom's book on the resurrection. She sat there for a while, finding there were no more questions really she needed to wrestle with. She'd read enough to understand. It came down to a very simple decision. Either she believed what she'd read in the Bible was true or she would choose to believe it was not true. Tom was right—the final step itself was pretty simple.

She set aside the book. She was surprised to find

there was comfort now, not fear, in the decision she had probed and thought about and weighed for weeks. "Yes, Jesus. I believe. The Scriptures are true." She spoke the words aloud, willing to accept this relationship as a conversation that would now go both ways. She believed Jesus meant it when He said He wanted a relationship with her. That He loved her. She was falling in love with Him in return. She had been for weeks, coming to love the person she'd met in the pages of the Bible.

She wasn't sure what else to say to God, but Tom had suggested she just say what was on her mind. "I'm grateful you had Tom risk inviting me to church even when he knew he would likely be turned down. I'm grateful you made him a patient man, willing to give me space and not push as I sorted this out in my own mind. I'm sure it hasn't been easy on him, as he waited and hoped I would ask questions of him, only to find I would approach this my own way. Tom's a good man who loves you. I suppose you know that," she added, smiling.

She thought about what she'd said to God and decided she didn't have anything else to add. "That's all I've got to say at the moment. So, now what?"

She picked up the Bible and was content to turn back to the first pages of Luke. In a matter of weeks

God had managed to make clear to her what Christianity was about. He would sort out for her what came next, just as He had sorted out the details of this discovery so far. She knew life would be different from this day on. And for once that didn't scare her. It felt like the first day of a new adventure.

Her family needed to see what she had found. None of them had considered God in a serious way before. They needed to believe too, not only so they would be in heaven with her one day but also so they didn't have to live life on their own, without God to help them. She wondered what their questions would be and how they would respond. They would listen because they loved her, but they would have to weigh the evidence and each make up his or her own mind.

As important as Tom was becoming in her life, her relationship with him had begun only this year. The O'Malleys had been closer to her heart than anyone else for two decades. She thought about the Fourth of July and how many big topics she would be bringing with her. *Christianity*. *Boyfriend*. They would wonder what was happening to her all the way down there in Texas. They'd be happy for her because she was happy—they were loyal that way. *Puzzled but happy,* she thought. She could work from that starting point.

9

Jennifer could hardly wait to tell Tom her news. It was bubbling up inside her so much she knew her smile was going to draw his comment sooner versus later. He carried in his groceries that afternoon while she held the door for him, and she followed him into his kitchen. She leaned against the island countertop, watching as he put vegetables in the crisper drawer. "I believe the Bible is true," she said quietly.

He looked around so fast he nearly dropped the package of carrots. "Really?"

She nodded.

He left the refrigerator open, the carrots on the counter, and swept her up in a hug even as he laughed. "That's wonderful news, Jen. When did this happen?"

"This morning." His smile was so big and his expression so full of joy—she couldn't remember seeing him this happy.

"What was the final tipping point?"

"'Jesus loves me, this I know, for the Bible tells me so,'" she replied, quoting the song. "I finally figured out what even my patients have been so confident about. *Jesus loves me. This I know.* And because that is true, the rest of it can be true." She paused a moment, gathering her thoughts. "Which is easier, to just say the words *I love you*, or to mean it and act on it? I figured out Jesus really meant it, and He died for me. They're not just words."

"I'm so glad, Jen."

"Are you crying?" She leaned back to look into his face.

He blinked fast. "I'm considering it. This means an awful lot to me."

She was beginning to realize that. "Maybe I should have told you later tonight."

"No way. This errand stuff can wait. We should celebrate."

"I thought you could make popcorn, and we'd watch a movie—something simple. You need to put your groceries away first. Your ice cream is melting."

"We could do that. I'm just so glad . . ."

"I like you happy like this. I didn't expect this to be your reaction."

"Okay, so I'm kind of emotional about stuff I really care about." He eased back a step and rescued the ice cream. "A good movie, popcorn, maybe a walk—our standard threesome."

"I like it." She picked up an apple from the bowl on his counter. "I've decided one of us needs a dog. We walk too much not to have something that's four-legged scampering along with us. Most everyone we pass is walking a dog."

"Where did this idea come from?"

"My kids. What do you think?"

"Right now I think you could ask for an elephant and I'd try to accommodate you."

She laughed and picked up his car keys. "I'll go get the milk from the car. I think I'm a distraction. You just put the ice cream in the refrigerator rather than the freezer. I'm going to have to remember this."

Tom stretched out on the floor beside the couch and shared the popcorn bowl with her while the movie previews crossed the screen.

She leaned over the couch cushion and looked down at him. "Could you be the one to baptize me? The idea of getting dropped while leaning back in a big pool of water isn't exactly the way I want to make this public confession of faith the Bible talks about. No offense to our pastor, but I know you."

"I can do that."

"It's not against the rules or something?"

"Or something. I'll have you know I've baptized three people, and not dropped a one of them. I'm an old hand at it."

"Other girlfriends?"

He couldn't help laughing. "You're never going to give up until you get an exact count, are you?" He held up two fingers. "I've had two serious girlfriends. Marie is now a physician in New York; Amy is a photographer in Colorado. Both still like me, and both broke up with me because they met someone else they liked more."

She considered that. "So what's wrong with you I don't know about yet?"

He threw a piece of popcorn at her. "Since it was all the way back in high school and junior college, probably nothing besides the fact I was too tall." He shifted his head and smiled up at her. "I hit medical school and the only thing I saw for about a decade was books and more books and the underside of a pillow while I tried to get some sleep between intern shifts. After that I discovered I was kind of selective. One-time dates do not count. I figure I was waiting on you."

"I'm going to skip that last point for the moment," she remarked, reaching into the popcorn bowl. "You do realize you've never invited me on an actual date, don't you?"

"I realize."

She dropped a handful of popcorn on him. "We'll have to talk more about that omission after the movie."

"Yes, ma'am."

They'd met with the pastor and planned the baptism for Tuesday, the first evening they both had off work, inviting a few friends and Tom's parents to meet them at the church. Jennifer felt excited about what was coming and nervous at the same time. "What if I fumble the words?"

"You're not on a microphone or with a big crowd,"

Tom reassured. "Just friends, family, and lots of people thrilled for you. If you need to repeat the words a couple times, it's not going to be remembered."

He straightened the white robe she wore over her sweatshirt and jeans. "I should have suggested a lighter-weight shirt. Just remember you'll feel heavy as you come up out of the water, and these robes tend to bunch up when they get wet, so move slowly until you have your balance again."

"Okay."

Tom nodded to the pastor's wife, who had come back to assist them. She whispered to the music minister that they were about ready, and they heard the song that was playing change. In another minute, they would be cued.

Jennifer entered the baptistery with Tom behind her. The water was warm. She was relieved at that fact. It was a deep pool, but not that big. She judged the distance and took a safe stance far enough toward one end so she wouldn't have to wonder about hitting the side.

"Don't be nervous," Tom whispered. "I'll lead with the words, so just look at me."

"Okay." She took a deep breath and tried to relax. It was a good nervousness, but she wanted her voice to be clear.

Their pastor wasn't on a mic, but they could hear him finishing his remarks. "This is one service of baptism I wouldn't want to miss for anything. Tom has been a part of this church family for a long time, and his firm faith and love for God warms my heart and challenges me. And I think Jennifer has seen some of the same things in him. It's a delight to gather together to hear her decision and share with her this day that marks the beginning of a new life."

Tom squeezed her hand. "Ready?"

She nodded.

The privacy curtain slid back. Jennifer scanned the faces of friends who had come to bear witness to this moment, sharing the joy that was present on their faces, and then looked back at Tom.

He led her through the simple words.

"I believe that Jesus is the Christ, the Son of the living God," she repeated, certain now they were true and all that Jesus promised was about to become hers.

"Jennifer O'Malley, on the confession of your faith before these witnesses, I now baptize you in the name of the Father, and of the Son, and of the Holy Spirit, that you might receive the forgiveness for your sins, the gift of the Holy Spirit, and the promise of eternal life," Tom said, his voice confident and sure.

Her grip tightened on Tom's forearm, she took hold

of her nose as he had cautioned, and he lowered her back into the water. The water closed over her head, the sensation of falling was checked by the strength of the man holding her, and then she was being lifted up.

As she came up out of the water, she heard a chorus of amens from those who had come to witness the moment. She blinked away the water, then smiled up at the man who held her. Tom smiled back. He made sure she had her balance before moving his hand supporting her. She released her hold on his forearm. "I wondered if you were going to drop me there for a moment," she whispered.

"Not a chance, precious. Not a chance." He looked proud of her. It had been a long time since a man other than family looked that proud of her. He nudged her to the left. "Look over at Joan."

She turned and smiled for the photo she'd asked for—a record of this important day for her album. "Thanks."

"You're very welcome."

The curtain closed around them as the music for the song Jennifer had requested began.

Tom guided her up the steps and out of the water. In the privacy of the baptistery area, she took the offered towel to wipe her face and accepted the dry robe. Tom draped a second towel over her wet hair.

"Go change. I'll meet you back here and we'll have Communion together in the chapel."

"It will be a few minutes."

"We've got all the time in the world tonight."

"I thought I would feel different or something," Jennifer mentioned as they walked along a familiar block, almost to the downtown fountain they'd visited on their first evening together.

Tom looked over at her. "How do you feel?"

"Happy."

"I'd say that's a strong enough emotion for the moment."

"It's nice, knowing Jesus loves me, really knowing it deep in my heart."

"You're loved, Jennifer. Enormously. By one who will never withdraw that love. There's nothing else like this peace. The Bible says even death has now lost its sting. It's just stepping from this life into Jesus' presence."

"It's hard to get my mind around the idea of what eternity will be like in heaven."

"Enjoyable," Tom replied, smiling.

"You'll pick me up for church Sunday?"

"Bright and early," he promised.

She dug change out of her pocket. "I think I'll move up to tossing quarters tonight and thrill whoever scoops up the money out of the water every week."

Tom opened his hand and showed her a bankroll of coins. "I got you Texas state quarters. I figured you could use ten bucks for something absolutely frivolous but celebratory tonight."

She laughed as he broke open the roll and dumped them into her hand. She walked around the fountain and studied where coins had already bunched. "Do you think God would mind if I started listing all my patients and praying for them to get well?"

"I think it would be a prayer that would bring joy to God's heart. He likes healing people, Jen."

"Will He make me a better doctor, do you think?"

"I think He'll fulfill the deepest wish of your heart, and do it for no other reason than it makes God happy to bless you."

"I wish I'd made this decision years before."

"You've still got a lifetime to fully enjoy it."

She trailed a finger through the water. "The other O'Malleys need to believe too, Tom. That's the deepest wish of my heart right now. And I'm not wise enough to help them with the decision—not the way you helped me."

"God laid the groundwork for you. Trust Him to do the same for the other O'Malleys too. He loves them even more than you do, if that's possible."

"I'm glad you're coming to the Fourth of July gathering and can meet them all."

"I was getting nervous that you wouldn't invite me, or you'd go on your own and meet someone you liked better or something."

She laughed. "Impossible. And I do like the fact you worry like that."

"It's called protecting my interests."

The cover on her own Bible was just beginning to feel broken in. Tom had bought it for her as a baptism gift. Jennifer set the book aside, having read for half an hour before turning in for the night. She was trying to absorb the words and become acquainted enough with the book of Luke that the verses would come easier to mind. Tom was familiar with this book in an intimate way and could describe passages in detail. To her it still felt so new, even after reading sections multiple times.

She found herself humming "Jesus Loves Me" as she got ready for bed. She had heard it from many of her patients over the years, and she'd learned the melody long before she had thought about the possibility the words might be true. Now it seemed like such a wise and wonderful song. Simple enough for a child, profound enough to capture so much of the heart of the Bible in its opening phrase. "Jesus loves me, this I know, for the Bible tells me so. . . ." Tonight, the words wrapped themselves around her like a warm blanket.

She turned back the covers and slipped into bed. Tom had convinced her she was loved by God. And it made the idea of falling in love with Tom so much richer. They'd share a faith too.

She wasn't afraid of the idea of falling in love anymore. It had been a concern over the years, how to juggle being a doctor with being a wife and someday, hopefully, a mother. She loved kids. She wanted to be a mom. But she'd trained all her life to be a doctor and she didn't want to set that aside. So she'd waited. Tom understood the dynamics and how important it was to her to be a doctor, the reason she loved kids. Rather than pushing them apart, it was becoming another connection they shared as he volunteered his time and got to know her patients. Tom was slowly convincing her it was safe to love him. She knew that was where he was heading, and she was willingly walking that road now.

For the first time in many years she was looking forward to not knowing how something would work out; it would take away some of the joy unfolding around her. For now, she was content to rest in the fact she was going to enjoy this journey with Tom . . . and with Jesus. It was becoming her special year to remember.

10

"Walk with me awhile," Tom requested. Jennifer obligingly slid her hand into his when he gestured toward the hotel gardens. Neither of them was in the mood to linger inside the dimly lit restaurant, and even romantic candlelight was not the most conducive to the relaxed conversation they were after.

Tom had said to dress up for this official date. She swirled her dress as she walked, watching it shimmer back and forth around her knees, and decided it had accomplished her hope.

"You look lovely, and you know it," he mentioned, looking amused.

She nodded her appreciation. "Consider this the final side of me you haven't bumped into before. At times I rather enjoy special nights like this and the dressing up involved."

He broke off something that flowered white and paused to slide it into the hair she'd pulled back with a pearl clasp. "It's been a nice night," he murmured.

"It has," she agreed. The gardens were private, the only sound the faint drift of music from the hotel across the grounds. They walked down toward the reflecting pool.

Tom pulled her to a stop by the roses and smiled down at her. "May I kiss you an early good-night?"

"I'd like it if you would," she whispered.

He cradled her face in his hands, taking his time, filling the moment with a tenderness that melted her heart. She basked in the feeling of being precious to him, enjoying both the care he was taking and the claim he was making as he kissed her. He brushed his thumb gently across her lower lip. "You are—" he leaned down and kissed her a second time, lingering to savor the feel of her and the taste—"a whole lot richer than I even dreamed."

She leaned into his hug and rubbed his suit jacket

button with her thumb. "Can we repeat tonight some-time? This has been very . . . nice."

"What were you going to say?"

"Fun. Enjoyable. Spectacular."

"I'll concur. Thanks, Jennifer."

She leaned back. "For what?"

"Not dismissing the idea of going out with me when you initially were faced with that decision."

She slowly smiled back. "I think I made a pretty good choice."

The relationship changed. It became easier to reach for his hand, to lean into an offered hug, to know there was a momentum to their time together now, and a new destination being explored.

One evening after he delivered her back to her home and prepared to leave, he quietly admitted, "I'm falling in love with you."

"I know," she answered from the security of their shared hug.

He smiled as he eased back. "That's all? Just 'I know'?"

She slid her hands up to hold his face still. "To me it feels . . . it feels like being in the sun after you've been stuck in gray, damp shade forever. Just being with you makes me content and so richly happy. I figured out some time ago it was because you loved me and were pouring it out in my direction."

He blinked back moisture in his eyes.

"Because I know you love me, it's making it very easy to accept that I'm falling in love with you too."

"You're okay with that idea?"

He wasn't taking anything for granted about her, and it made the soft question all the more special to her. "Before I met you, I would have been petrified with that idea. But now . . . now I'm growing more comfortable with the thought every single hour. You're swiftly becoming the most important person in my life outside of family," she reassured him.

"I can no longer imagine a day without you in my life."

"So where do we go from here?" she asked, not yet having sorted that answer out for herself, yet curious and secure enough to ask if he had.

He gently traced the curve of her cheek with his hand. "Forward, at the pace that seems right to both of us. I like the fact we're friends. There's no need or reason to rush past the enjoyment of this unfolding path with its twists and turns. We'll get where we are going together in the coming months. I haven't met your family yet, for one thing."

"There is that." She gave him another hug. "Thanks, Tom."

"For what?"

"Content, happy, settled, in love—it's a pretty big gift you just poured into my life in the last few months."

"I'd say it's been mutual." He kissed her a final time and stepped back. "Tomorrow I'll come find you at your office, and we'll go over to my folks or out to eat with friends—something."

She leaned against the doorframe as he headed down the porch steps. "A funny movie. I like to listen to you laugh."

He walked backward down the drive toward his car. "I'd say I like to watch you cry, but that wouldn't come out like I intended. I like to watch you get so involved in a show and care about even people who are acting that you get emotional about it. So maybe we'll do a double feature. One for both of us."

"Okay."

"See, all our decisions are going to be this easy."

She laughed, shook her head at him, and waited at the door until he was safely in the car and pulling from her drive. She was already looking forward to their movie evening together.

Falling in love was such a wonderful experience.

She smiled to herself as she locked up the house for the night, wondering why she had worried so much over the years about being the first O'Malley to be married. She was looking forward to the day Tom eventually proposed. She would probably cry all over him too, and the ring he chose for her.

A tap on her office door the next evening had Jennifer looking up with a smile from the chart she was updating. She expected it to be Tom. Her smile wavered as she saw her personal doctor in the office doorway. Their next appointment wasn't for another few days. Tina looked worried.

"Hi." Jennifer slowly put down her pen. "Come on in."

Her doctor closed the door behind her. "Your first tests are back. I'm sorry to bring news like this, Jennifer, but they show some troubling news."

Tina was carrying X-ray films and two reference volumes, both ones Jennifer had used in her own practice in the last few weeks. She stopped trying to think about what was coming. Instead she slowly nodded. "Tell me."

11

Tom pushed through the OR prep area doors back-ward to protect his well-scrubbed hands, whis-tling a tune he'd heard on the radio. Next up was an evaluation of a young surgeon doing a closure of a glass cut. The child was seven, the cut on his arm deep, and it would take a steady hand and some time, but it was well within the young doctor's proven range of skills.

"Tom?" Gina held out the wall phone. "Marla wants a word."

Surprised at the request, Tom diverted and walked over to join his surgical nurse. He'd have to rescrub, but Marla wouldn't have called the surgery suite if it wasn't important. "Yes, Marla."

"Jennifer called in and said she wouldn't be at work today. I don't know, Tom. She sounded like she'd been crying."

"When was this?"

"About twenty minutes ago. I've just finished shifting her cases for the day. The thing is, Veronica was scheduled to come in. Jennifer wouldn't miss an appointment with her without a huge reason."

"She didn't give any explanation?"

"No. That's what has me worried, Tom. This isn't like her. I just thought someone should know, since she doesn't have family in the area."

"Thanks, Marla."

Tom hung up the phone. An emergency page had cancelled their movie plans for last night, but he'd seen Jennifer on hospital rounds earlier that afternoon, caught her by phone at her office just before he went into surgery, and nothing had seemed unusual. They'd simply rescheduled their plans and moved them to tonight. He debated with himself just long enough to know there were some priorities that were going to clash in his life, and in this case it wasn't an even contest for which had to win. "Gina, is Kevin about finished with the skin graft?"

"He wrapped five minutes ago."

"Let's see if he can cover this evaluation for me. If not Kevin, ask Nathan to step over and handle it. And we may need to bump my one o'clock to after four p.m."

"Jennifer?"

"I don't know. I'm heading over there now. Call me if the world falls apart here; otherwise I'll be back as soon as I can."

Jennifer was sick? Something had happened to one of her patients? To someone in her family? Tom listened to her phone ring as he drove, and he wanted to toss the phone across the car when she didn't answer on either the house line or the cell phone she carried with her everywhere. He'd already paged her and hadn't gotten a reply. Tom turned onto her street, seconds later pulling into her drive. Her car was there.

He vaulted up the porch stairs two at a time. He knocked on her front door but got no answer. The door was locked. The windows didn't show him much beyond curtains. He searched the pot of cactuses and located the key she'd shown him hidden there. He unlocked the door. "Jennifer, it's Tom. Are you home? Are you okay?"

He strode through the house, feeling a growing sense of panic. She wasn't curled up on the couch fighting a headache or in the bathroom feeling sick. He headed upstairs.

"Jennifer?" No answer.

He backtracked, spotting color where it shouldn't be. She was in her office, sitting on the floor, leaning against the wall between the bookshelf and the file cabinet. A half-empty Kleenex box was beside her, the quilt from her bed had been pulled into a mound around her, and the phone cord twisted around her fingers. She looked up at him. Tears were streaming down her face.

His heart stopped. And a new litany of terrors swirled through his mind. Someone had gotten into her house and hurt her. Someone in her family had died. The worst of the worst possibilities slammed into him in the same heartbeat. He pushed aside the desk chair to reach her. "Honey, what's wrong?" He knelt in front of her.

She wrapped her arms tighter around her knees and shook, sobs the only sound she made. He forced her chin up to see her eyes. "One of your kids died?"

She wasn't even close to being able to answer him. He sat down heavily on the floor beside her and tried to wrap his arms tight around the bundle of quilt and woman. He didn't know how to help her or even how to try. He rested his head against hers and felt her tears drenching his shirt. He'd never in his memory seen someone so achingly hurting as Jennifer was right now.

"One of your family?" he whispered.

"I've got cancer, Tom. Late stages, malignant, around my spine and already touching my liver."

Her whispered words sliced into his chest like a knife. His breath didn't go down right.

"Tina broke the news." Her hand shook as she straightened her fingers against her raised knee and the fabric of her jeans. "That stupid backache I've had for months, that . . ." She started crying again.

He leaned his head against hers and closed his eyes.

"I did okay, last night, after she first told me. I really was all right. And then this reaction started in this morning, and it just won't stop."

"She told you last night," he murmured, shocked it had been twelve hours ago or more and Jennifer hadn't called him.

"I'm scared, Tom."

He cupped her face with his hands, searching for signs of pain, for signs of courage, for signs of the will to fight this. And what he saw frightened him. The shock in her was so intense and deep. "I love you, Jennifer." His hand shook too as he brushed her hair back from her face. "I love you. This won't touch that fact. We'll talk to the doctors. We'll figure out how it can be treated."

"I don't want you to have to walk this path with me." The words ended with a wrenching sob.

He sorted her hands out from the covers in order to hold them, and they felt incredibly cold. He enclosed them in his. "It's not your choice. You won't walk through this alone." He refused to consider the idea.

"I'm just so scared," she whispered again.

He struggled to get his thoughts around what he had to do first. Get information, lots of information, and some plan that helped her—and him—get through this. "We need to go see Tina together."

She shook her head. "I can't. Not yet. Not today. I need the denial for another twenty-four hours, not the reality. I can't take hearing the words again. You can call her; I told her it was okay to talk with you."

He needed facts, and Jen was right. She wasn't up to hearing this conversation yet, was in no shape to handle it right now. He eased the quilt up around her, wondering if she'd been right here most of the night. "Rest here, just a little while more, then I'm tucking you in somewhere more comfortable and getting something hot to drink into you. I'll be right back. Okay?"

She nodded and lowered her head against her upraised knees. He ran a trembling hand across her hair, then rose and left her there.

He found a phone in her spare bedroom, called his own office, and had the call transferred to her doctor. "Dr. Landers, it's Tom Peterson." He sank onto the bedside and pulled out a pad of paper from his pocket. "I'm with Jennifer O'Malley now."

Jennifer wasn't where he had left her. The quilt had disappeared with her. Tom walked down the hallway, searching for her, and heard a faint noise from downstairs. He headed down.

He found her in the kitchen, quilt around her shoulders, trying to fix herself a cup of tea. He wrapped his arms around her from behind and hugged her, resting his chin on her shoulder to watch what she was doing.

"She told you."

"Yeah. I've got us an appointment to see Dr. Everett at four o'clock if you're up to it."

She leaned into him. "You've got surgery scheduled."

"Already transferred to my partners. That was the second call I made. Do you feel up to eating something? I could fix a sandwich for you to go with that tea."

"You're crying."

He could feel the emotions gripping his chest, and the tears coming despite his determination to be strong and not give her the depth of his pain to add to her own.

"You're going to make me start crying again too," she whispered, turning to face him and wiping away the tears on his face.

"We'll beat this, Jennifer. We will."

He could tell she was giving it her best to smile at him. "We'll try."

She was breaking his heart. And his own tears didn't want to stop. Tom gave up trying. He leaned down and gently picked her up, quilt and all, and carried her into the living room, to settle into the chair and just hold her. "Rest awhile, and then I'll fix us lunch and we'll go see the doctor together," he said. "By then maybe I won't be crying on you. I don't think you slept last night."

"Not much." She sighed and turned her face into his shoulder. "I'm glad you're crying for me. It makes me know again I'm loved."

Within minutes he felt her drift to sleep, exhausted beyond what her body could fight. Heaven was supposed to be very beautiful. He cried at the very thought that was where she might be going sooner than he could stand.

She slept, and she ate, and shortly before three he convinced her to shower and change and take time to find something warm to wear.

She wasn't in pain, she didn't look ill, but her day had just gone dark. He couldn't get a smile from her, even a sad one. His own heart was too heavy to be much help. That had to change, for more than anything he knew she needed someone to keep her spirits up. He felt so unequal to that task.

"Say you'll marry me," he said. "I don't want to wait."

"I can't—"

"No." He cut her off with a gentle hand against her mouth. "Marry me. The most important moment in our lives together is not going to be pushed off by an illness."

"If—"

He didn't let her put out the reasons to say no. "Jen, I love you. I have for weeks now. I've been shopping for a ring. Just say you'll marry me. If the service has to wait until an opening in the treatment schedule, then we can at least get started on the wedding arrangements now. Just don't break my heart by saying no."

"I don't want you to watch me die."

The whispered words were accompanied by fresh tears down her face, and they ripped a tear in both his heart and hers.

"You're the most precious thing that has ever entered my life, and I'm going to enjoy a lifetime of loving you. There's not an illness in the world that can't be fought by some means or another, and we will find that for you, no matter where we have to go and who we have to see. You have to marry me, Jennifer. Please."

She rested her head against his chest. When she looked up at him, she struggled with her words, and her eyes overflowed with more tears. "I can't answer you right now, Tom. I'm so, so sorry. I just can't answer you right now."

And because he was afraid if he pushed any further, she would tell him no, he simply hugged her, held her, and tried to stay focused. "Let's go see what Dr. Everett has to say."

They were halfway to the hospital and the appointment with Dr. Everett when Jennifer put her hand on his arm and shook her head. "Pull over. I'm going to be sick."

As soon as he could, he pulled out of traffic, but she'd gone white as a sheet by then. She stumbled from the car to the side of the road and retched up what little he'd been able to convince her to eat.

He held her hair back and offered the napkins from the cup holder in the car. "I'm so sorry, Jen."

"Not your fault," she whispered. "Take me back home. I just can't do this today. Tests can wait one more day," she pleaded. "Just one more day."

He couldn't argue that point, not when it was obvious how hard the shock was still gripping her whole system. "We'll go back."

When they returned to the house, she was neither ready to be alone nor to have someone with her. Tom insisted on staying the night on the couch downstairs, and she didn't wave him off.

She wished she could stop his worry, all the pain this was causing him. She wished she could talk rationally about what this meant and what her plans should be. But it wasn't in her to have that kind of coherent discussion yet. She found sweats to wear to bed, for she was cold down to her bones, hugged Tom good-night, and went to bed to try to find the oblivion of sleep for a few hours.

The house was silent. Jennifer pushed back the covers and moved quietly, not wanting to disturb Tom if he was able to get any sleep at all downstairs. She stepped into the master bathroom and turned on the lights, shielding her eyes against the brightness until her eyes adapted. She studied her pale face in the mirror, her hair in matted strands needing shampoo, dark depressions under her eyes reflecting the lack of rest. She'd slept, but only in a fragmented way.

Not able to bear any longer the image she presented, she sat on the floor across from the sink and leaned against the wall. The spot wasn't totally private, but with the door closed it was as close as she could get tonight. The tears were coming again, welling up inside like a surging tidal wave.

"This is how you love me?" she whispered to God, starting to shake. She was enough hours past the news that the immediate shock was fading. Now the somber reality she had to face loomed before her, and with it was a wall of anger against what felt like a betrayal.

She leaned her head back to look up at the ceiling. "I don't understand, God. I don't understand. You just ripped away my life." She'd never felt anything so painful as this awful betrayal. Life itself was flowing away, and she couldn't hold on to it.

"You love me, and yet this is the first thing you put me through? *Jennifer, you're dying.* How could you do this to me, God? How could you do this?" Her frame shook, and her throat hurt at the words.

She rubbed at the tears streaming down her face. She fought sobs that were making it hard to breathe and tried to calm herself down. Blood dripped onto the bathroom tiles, and she wiped at the nosebleed. She tried to stand, but her shaking was too overwhelming, so she sat back down on the floor and leaned against the wall again, her whole body trembling.

She couldn't breathe.

"Don't, honey."

She heard the whispered words as Tom sat down beside her, but she didn't want to hear them. She didn't want Tom to see her like this, to watch her falling apart. She didn't want to hurt him like she knew she was doing by crying this way. She just couldn't take it. She couldn't.

He didn't bother to say anything else. He pressed a Kleenex into her hand for the tears, and a warm rag for the nosebleed, and just sat holding her while she cried.

She eventually took a deep breath and then another one, and let the explosion of emotions flow into the past. Her head ached. She sat still, considering the fact her eyes were swollen and her jaw hurt, and the floor was hard. Tom's arm around her hadn't moved in the last hour, and it was a comforting grip. She could feel herself regrouping, too numb to feel any more new emotions.

God, even if I don't believe, you are still God, she thought, knowing He heard her unspoken words. *It's an awful position I find myself in, unable to not believe in you now, unable to deny what I know to be true. You're still God. But I don't know how to trust you anymore. And if I can't trust you, I can't survive this. Why, of all things,* this? *Cancer—the one thing I know so well I can't have false hope?*

She thought about the months before her now, and she couldn't find anything but fear as she thought about what was coming. She'd watched too many patients over the years make this journey.

The one thing she sought in her patients more than anything else was hope, for from that came courage and the ability to face the decisions head-on. As awful as the medical options were before her, she had to find the ability and the will to fight. She just didn't know where to find that strength.

I came to know you, God, as good. Was I wrong?

Heaven tonight felt almost tangible. She was surprised to find that under all the shock still rested the certainty, *"Jesus loves me, this I know . . ."*

Somehow God was still God even in this. She knew it, as firmly as she did anything else about life. The truth was still the truth.

She drew a breath. For the first time since the news came, she felt decisions beginning to form.

I'm not going to pull Tom down with this, or my family. Even when the days get incredibly hard, I'm going to try to protect them from the worst of it. I have to. I can't let this destroy their lives too. I love them, God. I have to protect them somehow. That's likely going to be the last thing I can do for them.

She struggled against new tears as she thought about the future, about the odds this could be beaten, the odds it could not. Somehow there had to be optimism if she was going to walk this road, and she didn't know where to find it.

"Jesus loves me, this I know, for the Bible tells me so . . ."

"Please make me well, God. Please." The prayer was more broken than a whisper.

She turned and studied Tom, asleep as he sat beside her, his body forcing what his mind had refused to let him do, sleep. She wanted to marry Tom and enjoy life with him. She had to find the courage to live the life she did have as full and deep as she could. She slid her hand into his.

"Tom, it's dawn."

12

Jennifer hesitated in the kitchen doorway, watching Tom fixing breakfast. "Good morning."

He looked over, and she was relieved at his smile. "I fixed you some breakfast if you feel up to trying to eat something," he offered, studying her.

"I feel pretty good, all things considered." She looked at the eggs now cooking. "I'm kind of hungry too, so I might try some of everything. They want another CAT scan, and Tina has set up an appointment for me to see Dr. Everett this afternoon."

He shut off the heat on the stove and came over to

her. He put his arms around her. "I'll join you for all of that if you will let me. My day is open."

She hugged him back. "I was hoping you'd say that." One decision she had made was that she wasn't going to push him away, not even when she might want to protect him from the hurt this was going to bring. She reached for his hands and tightened her grasp. "Will you marry me, Tom?"

The joy that filled his expression overcame the sadness of the day. "You know I will. Thank you, Jennifer." His voice broke on the words.

"I love you," she said, emotions overwhelming her words. "The cancer may in the coming days dictate my energy and what I'm able to do, but it won't dictate my life. I want to love you and have a good life with you. If you can accept the fact it may be shorter than either of us would wish, I would really like to marry you."

"We'll have that together, Jennifer. A very good life," he promised softly. "I already found an engagement ring almost as beautiful as you. And we'll go shopping so you can find a wedding ring for me." He leaned down to seal it with a kiss. "A short shopping trip."

She laughed. "I'm getting the better of the deal."

His smile widened. "I'm not so sure about that."

"The wedding date . . . we'll see where we're at once the doctors figure out what my options are."

He eased her into a more comfortable hug and just held her. She could feel his breath stirring her hair. "There are going to be options, Jennifer. There always are. Prayer works, and the will to fight, and we'll find the best doctors to consult."

"And if the prayer doesn't get answered?"

"God always answers."

"I wish I had your faith."

"It's been borne out of years of history like this. I trust God, Jennifer, for a reason. He's dependable in tough times like this. Maybe the answer will come through a miracle of sudden healing, or maybe it will come through the healing hands of good doctors. But it will come."

"What if He says no?"

"God loves you. It's His very nature to do good. He's not going to say no unless it is truly for the best, and I don't see how that could be. We've got a life together; you've got patients to love. For now, just do the thing right in front of you that makes sense, and let Him take it from there. There's going to be a way through this."

"At the very least," she said against his chest, "I'll be able to tell my patients I know what they mean when they talk about facing cancer."

He rubbed her shoulders and leaned down to kiss

her. "Breakfast, then the test, and then the doctor. The next step is to know the details of what we're dealing with. Then I'm taking you out to celebrate our engagement."

Jennifer closed the folder the doctor had given her and rubbed her aching eyes. She got up from the desk and walked through the quiet house to find her shoes. She'd promised Tom a call when she was ready to go for a late dinner. It helped, having the data in front of her. But it was grim, knowing she was the patient. The cancer was ahead of them. If it hadn't touched her spine, maybe it would have been a clean fight . . . but there would be no easy decisions among the choices of surgery, chemo, and radiation.

At least they had a plan for the next few days. Her doctor wanted a specialist at the Mayo Clinic to take a look at the tumor around her spine before they made final treatment decisions. So she'd fly to Chicago to see her family, tell them the news, and fly on to Mayo for a second opinion. She'd return to Chicago for the Fourth of July family gathering, and Tom would fly to Chicago to meet her there, meet her family. As much as Tom wanted to travel with her to Mayo, she'd convinced him she needed him to stay here even more, handling the details as her patients were transferred to seeing other doctors in her practice. The details were covered; now she only had to wonder at the outcomes ahead.

God, what about the other O'Malleys? How do I handle sharing this news with them? The conversation with God seemed to flow where it would tonight, the comfort tangible. The peace was returning, the shock of the last days fading. None of this made sense, but God was still there. Just knowing that was keeping her searching for answers.

"How do I simultaneously break bad news and also try to introduce my family to you? I've got to find the right words."

The other O'Malleys had none of that comfort she knew and would only feel the fear of losing her in death to a disease none of them could see and could do nothing to stop. For a family of high achievers who believed in working together to deal with any problem, cancer was going to strike hard at the very heart of the group. They would want to share the journey with her. Every moment of it. For that was what it meant to be an O'Malley.

She tried to decide which one of them would be the hardest to talk with and thought maybe it would be Kate. Start with her first? Tell them as a group? Every possibility presented its own unique problems. Tom, the cancer, God. She had to figure it out and get it right.

"I wish you had given me an easier job," she whispered to God. "I can't afford to get this wrong. I want them to know you. That's my heartfelt goal and the only way there is peace if the worst does come to pass." Heaven lasted for an eternity, and that understanding was a weight on her shoulders tonight. Her family needed to believe.

Jennifer thought it might be better to simply start with the news about Tom and her engagement—the good news—then turn to the more difficult subjects. She looked at the ring Tom had given her, turning it to admire the diamond and the elegant swirled gold. He'd gone for classic and beautiful. She smiled just looking at it. She was going to love being his wife one day. It was time to get to Chicago and then Mayo and get through this journey. She wanted the joy that waited when it was done.

She picked up the phone. She was ready to celebrate her engagement and kiss her guy. He loved her. She deeply loved him. They would figure out how to get through this together. "Tom, I'm ready."

Author's Note

Jennifer's story continues throughout the O'MALLEY series. Her arrival in Chicago, as well as Tom joining her for the Fourth of July family gathering, can be found in *The Negotiator*, Book One. I hope you enjoy the entire series.

Dee Henderson is the author of seventeen novels, including *Full Disclosure*, the acclaimed O'MALLEY series, and the UNCOMMON HEROES series. Her books have won or been nominated for several prestigious industry awards, such as the RITA Award, the Christy Award, and the ECPA Gold Medallion. Dee is a lifelong resident of Illinois. Visit her at DeeHenderson.com.

If you enjoyed *Jennifer,* you may also like...

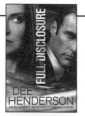

Midwest Homicide Investigator Ann Silver appears out of nowhere and drops the best lead on a serial murder case that Special Agent Paul Falcon has had in years. But is he ready for this case's secrets—or this woman's?

Full Disclosure by Dee Henderson
deehenderson.com

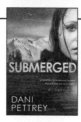

Amidst painful memories, Bailey Craig has reluctantly returned to her small Alaska hometown to bury a loved one. But when dark evidence emerges surrounding the death, can she and a former flame move beyond the hurts of the past to catch the killer—before Bailey becomes the next victim?

Submerged by Dani Pettrey ALASKAN COURAGE #1
danipettrey.com

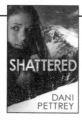

Piper McKenna would be overjoyed at the sight of her estranged brother Reef—if he wasn't covered in blood. She knows he's innocent. But when Reef is arrested for the murder of a fellow snowboarder by one of her oldest friends, can they discover the truth before it's too late?

Shattered by Dani Pettrey ALASKAN COURAGE #2

BETHANYHOUSE

Stay up-to-date on your favorite books and authors with our *free* e-newsletters. Sign up today at bethanyhouse.com.

Find us on Facebook.

Free exclusive resources for your book group! bethanyhouse.com/anopenbook

If you enjoyed *Jennifer*, you may also like...